The Gate of Paradise

Other Books Available from Blair Mountain Press

In Praise of Motels
The Silence of Blackberries
The Helen Poems
A Doorkeeper in the House
Idol & Sanctuary
The House
The Creek

The Gate of Paradise

a novel

Victor Depta

Blair Mountain Press

Blair Mountain Press
P.O. Box 147
Martin, Tennessee 38237

Copyright © 2000 by Victor M. Depta

Publisher's Cataloging-in-Publication

Depta, Victor.

> The gate of paradise / Victor Depta. – 1ˢᵗ ed.
> p. cm.
> LCCN 99-96563
> ISBN: 0-9666608-2-X

> 1. Fiction—Appalachian Region.
> 2. Family—Religion.   I. Title.

PS3554.E64G38 2000   813'.54

QB199-1578

To Robert Love Taylor, for his invaluable help during the writing of this novel.

Chapter 1

Ruby dug a Lucky Strike out of her crumpled pack and, in the heat of the day, wished to god she had a beer, an ice-cold Strohs. Not that she could drink on the porch, not in front of Deborah, though she could practically see one on the banister in front of her, the dark brown bottle with the slender neck, the label with the gold lettering, the slow trickling beads, which led her to think of the Ecco Pool Hall. She wanted to picture William sitting beside her in the booth, her hand on his leg, the profile of his handsome face, his union talk while she sat quietly, almost lazy but for the sweet, humming tenseness of her body, the anticipation of home and the bedroom. But William was gone, long gone, so the Pool Hall and the juke box excited her in a different way—mysterious and dangerous—the good-looking men she took to the tiny, cramped room at the hotel where she stayed during the week, the aimless romance like a druggist's potion which she gulped straight from the vial, as if to spite William and the world in her languorous rebellion against the ordinary.

Ruby knew the truth about herself, and it was that the moon, the sun and the stars were her guardians; they danced with her at the Pool Hall, and lay with her in her bed. Other people weren't stupid, necessarily, or so many fence posts and stumps, but they were deficient in what she had. They lacked what she knew in her flesh and bones, which was that her very self was a stream out of which she climbed, and to which the world came to drink and dampen its brow, to strip to its nakedness and bathe, to fondle and swell, to enter flesh and sweet oblivion. Ruby knew what love was.

She lit her cigarette and threw the match over the banister. A noise from the creek caught her attention. It was Keith. He must be building another dam. He, at least, was getting some fun out of living at the head of a hollow, miles away from anybody, the only neighbors being the crows and the hoot owls, their cawing and hooing the loneliest sound she had ever heard and could barely put up with. It wasn't that she didn't love her boy, more so now that he was getting older and could look after himself, but whenever he came to mind so did William, and the memories stung. William wanted his sex when she was as far as eight months along, struggling with shortness of breath, leg pains, back aches and hemorrhoids. He wanted it from behind, which she never liked much, anyway. And afterwards he demanded it when she was still torn and sore. When she didn't comply, he held her down and put cigarettes to the inside of her legs and her belly. He griped when she tried to nurse the baby; and when her nipples abscessed and all she had was blue john, when the baby cried, nearly starving to death, he called her a worthless mother and a stupid bitch. He slapped the child if it whined while they were having sex, or when she paid any attention to it at the dinner table. When the child started to walk, he slapped it away from everything, even the table legs. Then he nearly beat it to death before he took off, never saying a word, nothing, not about joining the Army, or anything. When Ruby glanced at her son, that is what she saw in addition to his blue eyes and shock-white hair. Keith looked too much like his daddy.

Anyway, he had Franklin to play with, if a six-year-old and a grown man could be called buddies or pals or whatever, considering that Franklin hulked over him like a hickory tree over a lilac bush and was dumb as a coal bucket, and epileptic, to boot. Not to mention that he had yellow teeth and was stubble-bearded, that his callused hands were flat, his fingers broad, his nails ragged and dirty. Ruby sized up a man in relation to how he would feel against her body, and Franklin wouldn't do. Besides his hokey appearance, he sulked. But she was grateful that he looked after Keith and kept him company.

3

Her cigarette made her mouth dry, and for some reason or another she couldn't keep from getting the paper wet, or keep shreds of tobacco from sticking to her lips, which she had to pick off or lick onto her tongue and spit out. Her mother complained about the way she nigger-lipped her cigarettes and wouldn't smoke after her when she butted one. Damn. Ruby could never think of her mother without irritation, and the butted cigarettes was just one example in a million which she carped about. One of Leah's constant complaints was that Ruby worked at the hotel. Her biggest complaint, however, was William, how Ruby had let him traipse away scot free.

Ruby was at the point of getting up for a glass of water, or maybe a cup of coffee, when her mother came onto the porch. Ruby slouched languorously in her rocker. She twisted a lock of her black hair around her finger, pulling it to her throat and letting it spring back into place. She was proud of her curly hair and her pale skin. She always wore a long-sleeved shirt and a straw hat when she worked out-of-doors. She didn't make an issue of it; she just did it. With a touch of powder, her face was white as cream.

"What are they doing in there?" she asked.

"Jawing, as usual," answered Leah, who sat in one of the rockers and strained her head forward from her scrawny neck. "And I want to talk to you about William. He's in California."

"No, Mommy," said Ruby, "that must be somebody else they was talking about."

"I reckon I know what I heard," said Leah. "It was William. Them brothers of his, and I don't know who all, are already back in Coalton, but William stayed in and got shipped to somewhere in California."

"Did they say where?" Ruby asked.

"You know them Brouseks as well as I do," Leah answered. "You don't expect nothing out of them, the tight-lipped hunkies."

Ruby slackened further into her rocker, evading her mother's words by going limp. She let her hands dangle at the ends of the rocker arms. She stretched and spread her legs a bit. She couldn't understand how her mother, in her forties somewhere, could look so wrinkled and old, her small face like a crab apple, a mean shriveled one, churlish and spitting nails. Ruby knew that she would never look that old, or that ugly.

"Besides," said Leah, "it wasn't the Brouseks I got it from, but from Wade—"

"Wade?" said Ruby. "I ain't seen him since we lived on Hereford Creek."

"Never mind Wade," said Leah, "and never mind Hereford Creek, either. We should of never moved up there. You messing around with William and that bohunk crowd, and what'd you get for it, a husband run off and you stuck with a snot-nosed brat. Where is Keith, anyhow?"

"Down at the creek," said Ruby. "And Keith's not a brat. He's mine. Anyway, William went to the war."

"Not before he run off first. I'm taking you to Riverton. There ain't no war going on now, and we'll get the FBI on his sorry ass."

"Ain't no need going to Riverton," said Ruby.

"No need!? He up and deserted you! Lord god, he must be the Devil hisself. He's got me talking nasty."

"There was a war," said Ruby, "and he went to it."

"And how come you ain't got no allotment checks? How come you never got no letter or nothing? You told me yourself he said, as clear as day, that he might have been cut out to be a coal miner but was sewed up wrong. And what about him beating Keith with that stick of stove wood?"

Leah's comments made Ruby nervous. The half-truth, that of William going to war, she stretched like fog after an evening rain which covered the daylight fact that he had beat her child half to death and then abandoned her. She turned away from her mother and stared at the path, at the tree line along the creek, at the mountain on the other side. In the years of William's absence, she had come to think of his leaving as a necessity and had almost convinced herself of the delusion.

"Is there any coffee?" she asked.

"Yes," Leah answered. "I had Franklin start a fire for a pot."

"I think I'll have a cup, then," said Ruby. "You want one?"

"Yes, if that sister of mine ain't poisoned it."

Ruby went inside and Leah sat on the porch by herself, rocking so determinedly that the rungs squeaked. Of all her children, Ruby was the worst. Not that she was a hussy, though word was getting around, and Leah knew because some of the godly told her, or hinted at what they might otherwise have kept their mouths shut about, since that sort of thing isn't ordinarily told to a mother, but Leah was so righteous a preacher that she'd condemn a child of hers as quick as she would a cannibal, and the godly knew it. But it wasn't that about Ruby. No. It was her do-less-ness, her way of sinking into herself when a subject came up she wanted to avoid, not quarreling or arguing but sitting there stupid as a china doll fiddling with its black hair. Hair didn't mean nothing to God, and neither did lipstick or powder or rouge, which Ruby used way too much of, and neither did flowery dresses or what was under them. The thought of what was under a dress suddenly made Leah flush, made her nauseous, nervous and feverish. Who needed a husband, anyway? Nobody sure needed hers, not George, least of all not herself and hadn't for years, more years than she could count. But Ruby. She wouldn't break under a righteous will. She bent like a willow branch, but that was it, just bend and spring back.

7

Ruby returned to the porch with two cups of coffee. Her Granny Deborah followed her directly and settled into a rocker.

"I guess, Mother," said Leah, "that you were in there talking about me."

"We wasn't," said Deborah. "Me and Vida was cleaning the flour bin and sifting the flour. I think I saw mealy bugs. In the corn meal, too."

"You're going to Riverton, daughter," said Leah, taking up the subject again with Ruby. "I'll see to it."

"There ain't no need," said Ruby. "I got me a job, and Granny is taking care of Keith."

"He ain't no trouble," said the old woman. "He'll do for you hardly before the words are out of your mouth. He's my angel, tow-headed as a angel, and his eyes are bright blue holes to see heaven in."

"Huh," said Leah. "I think he's albino, myself."

"Mommy," said Ruby, "he is not, only real fair."

"Me and Franklin can take care of him," said Deborah.

"Where is Franklin, anyhow?" asked Leah. "He vanishes ever time Vida shows up."

"No he don't," said Deborah. "He's around back somewhere."

"I don't see how you manage," said Leah, "what with two more mouths to feed."

"We're doing well enough, and Ruby helps along," said Deborah. She raised her thin, frail arms above her head. "God provides."

"No, Mommy," said Leah. "That's Franklin Delano Roosevelt. You ought to thank God for Social Security. You know if Daddy James hadn't of worked for the Land Company the years he did, you and Franklin wouldn't have none. And thank God for John L. Lewis, too, while you're at it. I don't like Ruby working in that hotel. The Devil flings enough temptation on the path, and it's for sure a woman don't need whole gangs of railroad men and drifting miners down there at Ecco."

"All I do is carry trays and wash dishes," said Ruby.

"Make sure that's all you do," said Leah. "You got the will of a wet mop."

"Ain't nothing wrong with Ruby," Deborah said. "She just ain't been delivered, yet."

"She needs to be delivered from William so she can marry decent," said Leah. "I don't see why them Brouseks ain't helping."

"I never asked for any help," said Ruby. "Besides, William wasn't raised good. I remember old man Ivan. He was mean. It's no wonder William run off when he was barely a man."

"He was riding the rails like a hobo," said Leah. "He should of stayed gone."

"Mrs. Brousek is real nice," said Ruby.

9

"Ain't got no fault with her," said Leah, "except she can't read the Bible and won't go to church. Says ours ain't her church, none of them. Catholic, hah! Ain't no Catholic church in five hundred miles of here."

Ruby wanted to get off the subject of William and his family, so she brought up a topic that her grandmother Deborah would take her side on.

"Where you going to this time, Mommy?" she asked.

"Over to Boone County, and then Raleigh," Leah answered.

"You off again?" said Deborah. "What does George think about that?"

"George is happy I'm serving the Lord," said Leah.

"You need to serve them closest to you, daughter," said Deborah, her small dark eyes narrowing in her skeletal face.

"We need to spread God's ever word," replied Leah sharply, pressing her long thin lips together like a vise. "It's revival time."

Deborah let the subject go. She rocked herself, the toes of her slippers lifting slightly from the floor, the hem of her nightgown swaying, touching her shin bones and shriveled calves. She pulled the housecoat more closely about herself, lapping one side of it over the other on her sunken chest. Her hands fell slowly to her lap. They settled there, half open, her slender fingers like the claws of a dead sparrow. Her head tilted on her neck, coming to rest on the rung-board above the pillow, and then inclined toward her shoulder. Her hair was white, and so thin that her skull was visible. Her wrinkled face had the appearance of cold gravy. She dozed off and her mouth opened, her jaw askew.

"Mother's asleep again," said Leah. "Seems that's all she does any more. I'm going on back to the house, leave you and Vida to talk about me."

"Granny's just catnapping," said Ruby, "and we ain't going to talk about you. You'll know if your ears start burning. You want me to wake her up?"

"No," said Leah. "She needs her rest. I got to fix George and Josephine a supper to eat and pack my suitcase. You remember what I said about William and Riverton."

"I won't forget," said Ruby.

She watched her mother stride down the path and into the road, then disappear around the curve. The place was so quiet that she heard a bobwhite off in the field, a woodpecker, the chickadees. Across the creek, the mountain rose in a narrow flank of ridge. A black vulture was circling in the distance. She looked at the sky, hazeless and blue as chicory flowers, the mounds of white, flat-bottomed clouds hardly drifting at all. But the more Ruby's surroundings drew her out the emptier she felt inside, so she shifted her attention to Ecco and the hotel, the steaming trays of food, the dining room clatter and din, the men's eyes on her, the jokes about getting in her pants. She carried trays among them with glazed eyes. She glowed as from a fever. Her cheeks flushed and her breath speeded up. And back in the kitchen, she washed dishes while thinking of Ralph, her newest boyfriend, who was not so much a person as a cured ham on legs, a do-less hanger-on who was black-haired, slack-faced, stoop-shouldered and paunched. She thought of the thickness between his legs and pressed her own together, crossing them as she rocked.

"Glory be to God!" shouted Deborah, startling from her sleep. "Hallelujah!"

"You all right, Granny?"

"Angels!" she said. "I saw them in the clouds, descending from the throne of God."

"You had a dream, I guess."

"No," said Deborah. "It weren't a dream."

"You want a cup of coffee?"

"Reckon not," Deborah answered, "even though the hotter it gets the colder I seem to get."

"It ain't too hot today," said Ruby. "It's pretty out."

"It's a shame about them daughters of mine," said Deborah, "fussing the way they do. Back in the kitchen a while ago, I thought Leah was going to snatch Vida's hair out. Leah's the oldest, you understand, and wants to boss. I never saw the beat for them two."

"For who?" asked Vida, coming onto the porch. "Me and Leah?"

Just like a turkey, Vida thought, lighting a cigarette and taking the rocker vacated by Leah. My sister's just like one, her beady little eyes and a beaked nose, and as likely to flare up and flog you without cause as that mean-ass bird. Meanest bird on two legs. And Leah's preaching was making a horse's ass out of the whole family, not that there was much for anybody to get high-toned and uppity about, to start with, but Leah's name was never mentioned without a snigger from somebody. A woman preacher in the family. Jesus. Vida knew she should keep her mouth shut when it came to Leah and her preaching, but she couldn't. The preaching was wrong, flat-out wrong, like a woman in a black suit and wearing a fedora. And her with George and a girl still at home to feed, even if George was as close to a corpse as a man could get and still breathe, and no wonder Josephine had gotten so feisty.

"Yes," said Deborah. "Nothing but quarreling."

"She starts it," said Vida. "Anyhow, your flour and corn meal's clean, Leah or no Leah."

"I could have done it," said Ruby.

"I know you could have," said Vida, "but I needed a chore to do, what with Leah here."

"Ruby," said Deborah, "I want you to pick up two half-gallons of milk at Vida's when you come back home at the end of the week, one sweetmilk and one buttermilk."

"Why can't Franklin do it?" Ruby asked.

"He just can't, that's all," said Deborah. "You can take them lard buckets with the lids on them in the morning. I wish we had a cow like we used to."

"Who'd milk it, I'd like to know?" said Vida. "Not Franklin."

"He would, too," said Deborah. "Don't you remember we used to have milk cows?"

"I guess," she said, dragging on her Chesterfield.

Deborah withdrew into herself. There was the old grief again. Hers and her daughter Vida's. Franklin. Franklin.

"Why don't you come to church tonight?" she asked.

"Christ almighty, Mother," said Vida, "when was the last time you saw me in church? Leah goes enough for us all."

"Preacher's coming to pick me up in his brand-new vehicle. But I can't get Ruby to go, either."

"I don't blame her," said Vida. "And speaking of going, I better get down the road. I got them heathen grandchildren to look after, not to speak of Danny, and there's supper to fix. Jake Hapney likes to eat."

"Well," said Deborah, "if you have to, and thank you, daughter, for cleaning my meal and my bins."

"Nothing to it," said Vida. "Bye, Ruby."

Vida fairly flew down the path to the road.

* * * * * * * *

Franklin had hunkered at the side of the house, first listening to Vida and Deborah in the kitchen, then shifting his attention to the front porch when they moved out there. He didn't strain for anything specific, the talk about Keith or otherwise. The boy, one day, was there, that's all, dragging behind at his mother's dress tail like a pup, and whining when she left the hollow. Franklin wasn't listening for information about William or anyone else. He was listening for harmony, the sighing wind, the flutter and call of birds, the distant murmur of creekwater. Disharmony darkened his mind and brought on the lightning in his brain. Leah didn't cause it. She was nothing more than a cat's hiss, an animal he could grab by the scruff of the neck and heft off the porch. But Vida's outbursts pushed him to the edge of a steep mountain cliff, where he reared up braying and terrified as a mule. He dogtrotted to the barn, and in the sun-shafted, warm dimness, he thought of Ruby's white skin. He lifted his penis out of his overalls and stroked it. Afterwards, he went to the chopping block.

* * * * * * * *

Keith had gotten bored with working on his dam. He lay on the bedrock, and the women's voices reached him. He listened for his mother's voice especially, the murmur and roundness of the sound like that of a mourning dove, but it was Leah's he heard most often, resembling a scrawny leghorn in the yard, squawking as it leaped to flog. Vida was raucous as a jay, while Deborah's voice was thin and clear, like a song sparrow. He was some distance from the house, and as the voices mingled with the gurgling of the water, he wondered drowsily where Franklin was. He drifted into a half-sleep.

He woke and lazily raked a twig across the water, herding the whirligigs. Their shiny black bodies skittered on the surface, so frantic and close-packed that their movement made a small whirring and clicking noise, and the surface was covered with tiny ripples. Their panic disturbed him so he let them go. He probed among the pebbles of the small pool, pestering the crayfish that either scurried backward or advanced menacingly, claws open and reaching upward. Dangling his hand in the water and holding it very still, he watched the minnows approach and nibble at his fingers and the fine hair on his wrist. But he couldn't catch them, no matter how quickly he jerked his hand about and closed his fist. Bored with trying, he rolled his bluejeans up past his knees, waded to the lower end of the pool again and picked up rocks, throwing them on his dam with a noisy splash. The bandage on his big toe unraveled and floated to the surface, white and blood-stained. He retrieved it, wrung it out, and put it in his back pocket. His toe began to sting, so he quit altogether and walked home.

He was slow and awkward, walking with the toes of his right foot curled upward, making his way over the outcrop and into the elms, sourwood and redbud which lined the creek, up to the johnson grass and purpletop alongside the road, where the dust was warm on his cold feet. He crossed the road and started up the path to the house, which stood on the flat of the sloping ridge, the porch high off the ground. He saw Franklin, and forgetting his sore toe, hurried to the woodpile at the side of the house. He squatted, watching him lift a block on end, split it with one blow, and then split the pieces to stovewood size. Keith raked wood chips with his fingers, building up his nerve to talk to Franklin; he inadvertently ran his fingers through chicken manure and wiped it off in the grass, hoping that Franklin hadn't seen. Gray, Franklin's half-breed dog—part collie and part German shepherd— lay panting at the edge of the house.

"Hey, Franklin, can I do that?" Keith asked after a deep breath.

"Suppose so," Franklin answered, straightening up and wiping his hands on his overalls.

Keith uprighted a block and raised the longhandled ax over his head. He swung as hard as the could and the head sank into the end. The block did not split; the ax was stuck. He tugged at it, toppling the heavy chunk and stumbling. He sweated and grunted. Franklin snickered and came to help, yanking the ax head out of the piece with one hand.

"You've not growed into it yet," he said, "but I got a hatchet you can use."

As they walked to the barn, Keith took his great-uncle's hand. He wasn't actually sure what relation Franklin was, or any of them. Ruby had tried to explain, when they first came to Deborah's, that Franklin was Vida and Leah's half brother, but how could Franklin be half of anything, and how come he was so much younger than his sisters? And what did *great* mean, as in his great-grandmother Deborah, his great-aunts Vida and Leah and his great-uncle Franklin? Great, like great big? And how could Leah's Josephine be his aunt when she was only sixteen, while Vida's Danny was his second cousin? Why second? He gave up trying. Most grownups were nothing but big hands that rumpled his hair and gripped his chin. Grownups leaned till their faces loomed before his, their grins huge, their teeth rotten and their breath foul. Their nostrils were hairy and black, their eyes round and blood-shot, their foreheads wrinkled. *Make a man out of him. He's whiter than a fish belly. Straw headed. A scarecrow.* But Franklin never clamped his chin or pinched his face. Franklin squatted on his heels or sat on a stump, and Keith stood beside him, watching him whittle, sharpen sickles and scythes, rinse salad greens and peel potatoes.

18

"Here it is," said Franklin, reaching up to pull the hatchet out of a beam. "I'll show you how to sharpen it, and how to hold the wood on the block."

Franklin took up a file and they returned to the woodpile. As he showed Keith the angle at which to file the hatchet, and as he guided his hand, he grinned with pleasure at the idea of teaching the boy a skill.

"Can I do the kindling from now on?" Keith asked. "Is that okay, Franklin?"

"Sure is," replied Franklin who, for the first time, began to see the boy on his side against them, Deborah and Vida and the rest. They set to work, and were soon sweating in the sun as the kindling and stove wood mounted up. "Best quit, now," said Franklin. "I got to help see to the dinner. The old woman asked for chicken, thinks the preacher might want some."

"Where do you want me to stack this wood?" asked Keith.

"Just carry some to the stove. We'll get the rest later on."

Keith dumped the wood beside the stove and hurried to the front porch. His mother was smoking a cigarette. He sat on the floor and leaned against the banister so he could see her face, her pretty mouth, her large brown eyes and black, wavy hair. He wanted to crawl up on her lap but was afraid to. She was gone so often, always some stuff about work at the hotel, her brothers and sisters and

19

them. They were like birds, like grackles in Vida's pasture, a flock of them whirling away, settling and whirling away again.

"You might get to see your Daddy, soon," said Ruby.

"My real Daddy?"

"I'm not promising," she said, "but you might. He was wounded over in Italy, but he's fine, now. Mommy said Wade told her he got a Purple Heart—"

"How'd he get a purple heart?" asked Keith. "Was he shot there?"

"No," she answered. "It's a medal for being brave. Your Granny Leah seems to think he's way out in California, but maybe we can find out different."

"What's he look like? Will he be wearing his uniform?"

"I suppose so," she said. "Your Daddy don't look like my family. He's blond headed. He's a good-looking man, real handsome. You got eyes like his, and hair, too."

"We going to live with him?"

"I don't know, honey. I don't reckon we will. Lord, look at your toe! Where's your bandage?"

"It's in my pocket."

"You better put it on," she said. "And I better help Franklin with dinner."

After his mother left the porch, the desire to be near her drew him to the rocker she had sat in. He got on his knees before it, reached under the arms to hug the backrest, and laid his head on the seat cushion. He was in bliss, and sighed. Suddenly he jerked his head away, his nostrils filled with a pungent musk. He scooted away, sitting on the floor again and leaning against the banister. He shuddered and closed his eyes, abruptly wizened beyond his years by the primitive scent which indicated, in his voiceless child's mind, that love has its awakening slap of betrayal, in his case an odor which wasn't bad or dirty, just very strong. He deadened his heart against it, against her, against whatever it was that drew her out of the hollow to Ecco. Tears came to his eyes, yet in his aged, unknowing self, he was sorry for her, although what he saw in his mind's eye was the water skimmers at the creek, how he had herded them, how they panicked.

The blighting incident passed as a solemn breeze through a hemlock. He left the porch and turned over a board just under the steps, poking at the pillbugs until he saw Franklin, at the side of the house, grab at a chicken. Crawling beneath the steps, he saw Franklin lunge and catch it by a wing as it squawked away. Franklin carried it to the woodpile, and Keith ran to watch. Franklin squatted. The hatchet rose and fell in a blur. Keith heard a *whack* and saw the white bundle of hen flapping jerkily in the air. It hit the ground with a thud and flopped about. Ruby came out the back door, carrying a bucket of scalding water, a paper sack and matches.

"You're supposed to kill the thing," she said, "not play around with it. You should of put it under the tub."

"It's done," said Franklin. "There it is."

"Granny wants you to help inside," said Ruby. "I'll pluck the chicken." She turned to Keith. "I asked Granny if we could have fried potatoes instead of mashed. You like them like that, don't you?"

"Real brown."

"Me, too," she said. "Throw that chicken head off in the weeds, will you, honey? And toss these feathers over the bank."

In the kitchen, watching his mother clean the chicken, he was amazed at the intestines, the lumpy matter in them, the craw with actual bits of rock, the giblets smooth as shiny-brown pebbles, the claws which she cut off and discarded, though he shrank a little as she severed them, and cringed as she cut the chicken up for frying. Franklin let him peel a potato. He wasted most of it, leaving too much flesh on the peel. Soon, the kitchen was filled with the odor of sizzling corn meal, hot lard and frying meat. Deborah made corn bread. Franklin hurried to the spring-house for the last of the milk. Keith was allowed to set the table, and as he laid out plates, he sighed contentedly. There was peace in the house; though, when Deborah asked him to say the grace, he gritted his teeth and mumbled. It irritated him that they should have to call on anybody when they had done all the work themselves. He munched on the hot corn bread, dark brown, crisp and greasy on the bottom, and washed it down with cold milk.

He would have liked more chicken, but Deborah was saving a breast for the preacher. Keith stuffed himself with corn bread and crunchy potatoes.

"There's rice pudding for dessert," said Deborah. "Fooled you, huh? You didn't think there was none. I ain't so old I don't know what a boy likes. It's in the cupboard."

Ruby filled bowls for them all, and Keith asked for seconds of the sweet, cinnamon-flavored dessert. Afterwards, when they were on the porch, Ruby brought coffee for herself and Deborah, then sat in the rocker to smoke her cigarette. She gazed pensively at the slope and the road. Deborah was tired after her effort and needed to nap again before church. They sat quietly. Franklin had a stupefied look on his face. Keith, lying on the floor, his head propped on his hand, pried up a splinter and gouged at the dirt in the cracks. The shadow of the house stretched down the slope, while the greater shadow of the mountain behind slowly overtook it. Already there was the slightest chill. The birds were making their plaintive, evening cries. Deborah stirred in her rocking chair, shivered, and wrapped her housecoat tightly around her chest.

"I best be getting ready," she said. "Ruby, you fry that piece of chicken. Keep the corn bread hot. Sprinkle water on it. Franklin, you can get the dishes. And Keith, you wash up. Get your neck and ears good, and wear your white shirt."

23

Keith grabbed the tin basin off the back porch and ran to the well. He opened the lid and let the bucket drop. After the chain stopped rattling through the pulley, he peered inside, but leaning against the wellbox made him fearful, as did the dark, silvery water. He hauled mightily, heard the thudding as the bucket rose, and was delighted when it appeared, clean and shiny, the water splashing on his forearms as he settled the bucket on the wellbox. He filled the basin and carried it to the porch, where Ruby brought hot water in the tea kettle. She lathered a wash rag and scoured his face. He howled when the soap burned his eyes, and groaned as she forced the rag into the whorls of his ears. She scrubbed his neck bright pink, rinsed and dried him. He was left dazed and tingling.

"You can't wear your brogans," she said. "Your toe's all raw, but wash your feet good, anyhow. Don't just wet them and wipe the dirt off on the towel."

"Do I have to go?" he asked, suddenly fearful.

"Yes. Granny wants you to."

"Why?"

"To keep her company, I guess," said Ruby.

"Well, I don't like it."

Ruby saw to the chicken and corn bread, then went to help her grandmother. Deborah was bent before the chifforobe, fumbling at the last buttons down on her dress. "Aggravating things," she said as Ruby stooped to button them. "Thank you, child. It makes me dizzy to bend over."

24

"There, that's it," said Ruby. "Let me help you with that belt, the thin little nothing. You want me to pin your hair up?"

"Would you, please?"

Deborah sat sideways on the bed. Ruby took a comb and bobby pins from the washstand. She gently combed from the front, covering the thin spot on Deborah's crown, and gathered the strands at her neck and about her ears, pinning her hair in a loose bun. She couldn't gather all the wisps, and they shone faintly in the evening light. As she brushed and straightened Deborah's collar, Ruby noticed the brown, wrinkled skin on her neck, and how thin her neck was. She noticed the freckles on her large ears, the thick blue veins at her temples. She leaned from behind and kissed her grandmother on the cheek. "How old are you, Granny?"

"Now that's a peculiar question," said Deborah. "What's a young thing like you concerned about us old folks for? We ain't hardly talked at all."

"I just wondered," said Ruby.

"Seventy. I'm seventy, borned in 1876, and I moved up this hollow in 1893, a bride at seventeen."

"Don't you ever get lonesome?" Ruby asked.

"I used to when James was alive," Deborah answered.

"James?" said Ruby. "Oh, you mean Grandpa?"

"Yes, my husband, James Waugh," said Deborah. "You weren't around enough as a child to have any memory. Funny, ain't it, to be more lonesome when he was alive than now when he's dead, though it's true. Oh, I smoothed all the edges off, like a worn-down set of steps. But I rankled, no doubt of that. Who wouldn't with a thing like Franklin in the house? I was dutiful, but it didn't amount to a puff of smoke. James was a stranger long before he drug Franklin home. And I took it out on the child. I know I did. I still do. I miss James like I'd miss a shed burned down, like a lost shovel."

"Granny!" exclaimed Ruby.

"It's true," said Deborah. "But I suspect you're the lonesome one, what with nobody living close by. The mines did that. Look at Leah and George. George moving hin and yon all of your all's life, each of you born on a different creek, up a different hollow, like ragamuffins, Charles and you and Josephine. Vida's children, too."

"You have to go where the work is," said Ruby.

"I imagine so," said the old woman. "Mercy, girl, that chicken might burn to a crisp. You best go see to it, and thank you."

"You're welcome, Granny."

Keith was helping dry dishes, and Franklin smiled at the way he set a plate on the table, dried one side, then turned it over to dry the other. Ruby laid out the food, lighted the kerosene lamp, and went to the living room to light the other. Their yellow, smoky glow was pale in the twilight. They heard the preacher's car on the road; and

Keith, like a wild animal, bolted through the back door and around the side of the house. From his hiding place he saw the Chevrolet stop halfway up the path. It looked to him like a huge, black beetle with silvery eyes and an ominous, leering mouth. The preacher got out and Keith heard the family on the porch.

"You going to church, Franklin?" asked Ruby.

"Going to walk."

"Keith can ride with me," said Deborah. "Howdy, there, Reverend Bledsoe!"

"Evening, Mrs. Waugh," the preacher said, coming up the steps. "You all ready for church?"

"We sure are," said Deborah, "but you got time for a bite, first?"

"I always have time for your chicken, Mrs. Waugh."

"Well," she said, smiling, "come on, then."

Keith slunk along the house and peered through the kitchen window, watching the preacher eat chicken and corn bread, talking with his mouth full, though Keith couldn't make out what he was saying. His greasy lips moved, and coffee dribbled on his chin when he drank. Ruby was washing the skillet, and directly Franklin disappeared out the back door and down the slope. Keith watched him fade in the twilight. When the others walked out to the porch, Ruby called, and Keith made his bashful way to the front. It was an agony to walk alongside the preacher, who had his hand at Deborah's elbow and was

27

helping her down the path. Keith was flushed and his ears buzzed. He heard his mother wishing them a good church service.

Franklin took the path around the hill so the preacher wouldn't see him on the road and leave him in the choking dust. Gnats moiled about his head, and he had to stop several times to wipe the spiderwebs off his face. His foot slipped once on a mossy rock, and he fell heavily on his thigh. To avoid Vida's house, he took the cow path on the far side of the pasture. He wanted to get to the church. He wanted to watch the old woman.

Keith, in the car, was attacked by the smell of fresh paint, plastic and rubber. The brown upholstery was rough against his hand and prickly through his britches as the preacher jarred in and out of the chuck holes. The trees looked eerie as the headlights swept over them, though the hollow broadened to include more sky as they neared Vida's, whose house was ablaze with lights. He saw bustling figures behind the windows, heard voices, shouts and laughter. Several women were standing on the front porch, including Della, whom Keith liked. Off to the side, a group of men were loafing in the yard. Children ran about, shrieking in high-pitched voices.

Vida glanced through the living room window and saw Keith in the car. She recognized him in the dimness by his hair, which lay on his head like an oversized, white cap and gave his face the appearance of a small wedge. Then a scene appeared before her more vivid than any dream: the cover on the hall table in her mother's house. Deborah had arranged it odd-ended so that the corners draped. She was placing her Bible on the table. Small hands reached up and tugged at one of the corners. Deborah turned and slapped the child directly in the face. Franklin. And then a strange gurgling sound rose out of Deborah's throat, a moan rising to a wail, which frightened Vida terribly, and then a similar shriek from Franklin. Vida jerked back from the window. Keith seemed to be looking at her. Damned kids, she thought. They sprang up like weeds, dirt common, and to give special attention to one was the same as grooming a gnat. Keith shouldn't be bothering her. He certainly didn't look like Franklin, and that dumb Ruby, asking why Franklin couldn't come get the milk.

Della and two of the women left the porch and climbed into the car. Keith's nostrils filled with the perfume of the two women, at first pleasant as roses and lilacs, but then smothering, mixed with body heat. Their voices were cloying, a babble of politeness to which Reverend Bledsoe responded with unctuous vanity. The tension was incomprehensible to Keith, who shrank against the door, and who was immensely relieved when Della reached across him and rolled down the window.

He leaped from the car as it pulled into the church yard. The excitement of the congregation, many of the members still chattering on the walk, affected him like

29

catnip does a cat. He raced along the white fence with outstretched arms, his hand striking the pickets. He ran back and forth several times before Deborah called. He went inside with tingling fingers. As he, Della and Deborah made their way to a pew near the front, he noticed Franklin taking a seat in the last row back.

The hymns were high-pitched and morosely paced. Reverend Bledsoe was an octave off key; the few other men in the congregation croaked hoarsely. The women wailed and their voices cracked. And to Keith the sermon was gibberish, one moment sweet as a mockingbird on a fence, the next like a hound growling over a bone. He leaned against his great-grandmother and dozed, waking only when the preacher neared the climax which, to Keith, sounded like Franklin with the stray cat. *Here kitty kitty.* Franklin had murmured and cajoled, followed by an impatient *Damn you to hell* as he threw the chicken bone at the wary animal. But Keith did understand the general drift of what Reverend Bledsoe was shouting about. It was sin, as when Granny Leah switched him for peeing in bed, though she yanked him out of sleep and into punishment so fast that the pain arrived before the comprehension did, and he hated her for it. He never peed on purpose, anyway, and with his child's intelligence he loathed himself for admitting that he was sorry. He was glad that he and his Mommy had left her house for his Great-granny Deborah's.

Deborah startled Keith by rising from her seat. She gripped the pew in front with one hand, and with the other she waved her handkerchief in the air. It looked to Keith like surrender in a Cowboys-and-Indians game. She began to shout, but not in drawn-out moans or in high, piercing wails. It was a song he couldn't understand the words to. It seemed to float over the congregation in a complexity of tones, the lower ones rasping with pain, or throaty and deeply sweet, those next like broken sobs, lengthened cries of farewell, and the highest ones warbled like cowbirds in the bushes, and babbled like the water over his dam. He listened in amazement. She was talking to God, of course, and that interested him about as much as saying grace at the table, but he was fascinated nevertheless, as the time when Franklin drew the curtain back from the window screen and held the lamp next to it, attracting the moths whose eyes turned fiery, with facets of red and orange as the lamp was moved toward them, but plain moths, scraping and flapping on the screen, when he moved the lamp away.

Franklin watched the old woman have her fit. She was helpless, then, taken up by a force like the one that came on him, that made him babble and foam as the lightning struck. When she sat down, he bolted out the door.

Keith was impatient until the altar call, when the voices turned sorrowful and plaintively sweet. They seemed like caresses, pleading with him to lie down, as if he were sick of a great deal more than peeing in bed, and that he should weep and cry out in pain. They would lift him up with their soft hands. But whose soft hands, he wondered. Not the preacher's, or the ladies who smelled like sweaty roses, or his Great-granny Deborah, who stroked his hair, kindly yet abstractedly, and was in some distant place by herself. And not his mother. He looked to the back of the church, but Franklin was gone. Della, who was almost certain that she was pregnant, since she'd missed her second period, took Keith's hand and held it.

Chapter 2

Ruby hated Sunday, especially the afternoon and evening, when there wasn't a bed to make or a dish to wash, which she didn't mind doing because she liked a neat, pretty house, but it was damned hard to dust when there was nothing to see by but a kerosene lamp, and mopping was out of the question. And the lamplight wasn't scary, exactly, but she was used to electric lights, everybody was, and it was only at Deborah's the power lines didn't stretch to, at the narrow end of nowhere up a hollow. Ruby was edgy, since she anticipated Ralph but wasn't positive he would show up. She brushed her hair and was pleased with the thickness, the black sheen of it in the chifforobe mirror, the way it lay against her smooth neck and alongside her cheek. She primped in the mirror, and as she did so her mind skimmed the past and lapped at the buttery cream, at the image of William as he leaned toward her, when his eyes were soft and his breath was sweet as mint. She remembered nibbling at the flesh of his mouth, and

how he trembled and surrendered to her. She also remembered when he seemed oblivious of her, when he
withdrew into himself, cold as a stone, or shouted something nasty or hateful. Yet those memories, too, were rich,
since she could admire his hard, stony profile, the hand-
someness of it, the way he frowned into the distance and
ignored her, since his surrender, when it came, was that
much more delicious, when he clung to her and fairly cried
out *I'm sorry, I didn't mean what I said, I didn't mean it.*
William always came back to her. He would come back to
her again, now that the war was over. She rubbed the
powder puff voluptuously over her throat, then pouted and
applied her lipstick. She heard the dog bark as she took
up the perfume bottle.

* * * * * * *

Vida came to the porch ready to squall. She liked to
squall; it made her feel good. Just as she was about to
open her mouth she noticed Ralph in the yard with Jake
and a couple of men on the midnight shift at Ecco. She
frowned heavily. It wasn't enough for Ruby to be getting a
reputation down at the hotel, and she knew well enough
what the case was because Jake hinted at the rumors as if
he were sending telegrams to everybody in the county, but
now she had to have men sniffing around at Deborah's,
which was the homeplace, Vida's and Leah's and the

brothers'—though they were dead—and it didn't need screwing in. Not that she blamed Ruby much for wanting a little, or even going at it as if the world were ending, since she'd had enough trouble out of William to drive any woman to distraction, but to settle on Ralph, that shiftless lummox who was hung like a stud horse—she knew he was hung by the jokes the men made about his pecker being big as a ball bat—and dumb as an ox, to boot, well, any woman in her right mind wouldn't any more look at him than they would a fence post. Ruby was a fool and that child of hers was as much as an orphan who saw its mother, maybe, three hours out of a week. And the obstinate little jerkoff wouldn't set foot down the road to her house. Franklin was no companion for a boy. She squalled, "Sally! Luke! You all get in here, it's darker than a nigger's ass. And Luke, where's Beulah's Pete at? Go find him!"

"Well, boys," said one of the miners in the yard, "we'd better head down the road. Number Nine's waiting for us on the mountain."

Jake wanted a drink and he wanted somebody to drink it with. "Ain't no hurry," he said. "Why don't we go in the house?"

"Can't, Mr. Hapney," said Ralph. "I best get back to the hotel. It's a stretch of walking out of here."

He left the yard before the other miners, and when he was some distance down the road, he crossed the field and backtracked, waddling through the brush, crawling under fences and over rock-piles. At the upper end of the pasture, as he was crossing over to the road, he walked broadside into Jake's horse. "God dammit!" he yelled as the horse snorted and trotted away. The hair stood up on the back of his neck. Once in the road, he scraped the manure off his shoes.

He was able to see a little better, what with the moon rising above the mountains. The branches along the road were a ghostly green, the tall woods purplish black. He hurried, with his haunchy need, toward the Waugh house at the head of the hollow. His urge, mindless as a whip-poorwill or a rasping katydid, took various shapes: a meal sack, flowery and smooth as a belly; the cleft of a ripe peach; the smooth forks of a beech tree; moss on a ridge. He lengthened his stride and felt the swinging and rocking at the inseam of his drawers, felt the lifting from his thigh, the tingling as his trouser-leg chaffed across the heft. When he saw the glow of windows, it rose beet-headed.

He turned up the path and Franklin's mongrel growled and leaped from the porch. It bounded down the path, snarling and barking. "Here, Gray!" Ralph shouted. "You dumb dog, you're about as crazy as Franklin is. Come here, boy!" The dog quieted and allowed itself to be petted. Ruby came to the porch. Ralph, as he climbed the steps, smelled her perfume, the strong candied musk of it, which did not make him dizzy, but nonetheless filled the cavity of

36

his head like smoke in a bee tree. Ruby smiled. He looked at her dark curly hair, her white face and red lips. "Evening, Ruby, how you been doing?" he asked.

"Okay, I reckon, and you?"

"I been thinking about you all day," he said.

"And I know what you been thinking, too."

"I suppose you do," he chuckled. "I brought a half-pint we can share."

"You did? Lord, how I could use a drink."

"I been saving it," he said.

Rather than take him to the bed she shared with Deborah, she led him to Franklin and Keith's room. Moonlight shone lead-gray through the window, and a bar of yellow light stretched across the floor from the kitchen lamp. They lit cigarettes and Ralph opened the whiskey. The first drink, like a fire in her throat, all fumy and oily, nearly gagged her. Ralph swallowed deeply, and then Ruby again. As the whiskey spread through their bodies, they sighed and kissed, facing each other slightly aside, she with her hand on his pants' front, he with his hand pressed between her legs. They heard the dog growl.

"Damn," Ralph whispered.

"It's nothing," said Ruby. "He does that in his sleep."

She unzipped his pants, and what was in her hand, then, was thick and grotesquely large, and with so much foreskin that, when she tugged it away from the head, the sac below dangled like a gourd between his legs. She leaned her head against his chest so that she could peer down. The thing was a wonder to her. Protruding from his trousers, it didn't seem a part of him, as his hands and forearms were, but a fleshy something separate from himself. She could respond to it and ignore his personality, or the lack of one. He moved in front of her.

"Let's get in bed," she whispered.

****

If people could have seen Franklin running up the road in the dark, they might have thought that he was scared out of his wits, but Franklin was running because he was happy. He had watched thunder and lightning descend on the old woman, had seen her tremble and throw her hands in the air, had heard her shout and scream and talk crazy. What he so often suffered, she suffered. He knew people thought he was dumb, but what they didn't know was how he kept the fits away, which as an actual plan was unbeknownst to himself, and that was to gauge his heart, to sense the beats in his chest and listen as they surged against his ears. When he hoed the beans and corn, when he chopped down a tree and sawed it for stove wood, when he hauled coal for the grate, when he scythed or carried water from the well to scrub the floors, when he washed the dishes and shined the pots, then the beats were comforting almost as sleep itself. But

38

he disliked talk; he disliked people. They always wanted him to listen, wanted him to be or to act in a way unaccustomed to himself, sometimes simply by unburdening their bundle of nerves upon him, and then he felt helpless and frightened. His heart speeded up and the ringing started in his head. So, a long time ago, he had stopped listening. He turned away, and those he turned away from thought he was a moron, but he wasn't. He knew he wasn't a retard. Keith knew he wasn't. Keith was the only one who really knew. And maybe Ruby. Franklin turned off the road and raced up the path. Gray stirred under the porch, growled before he recognized his master, then went loping down the path toward him. Franklin stooped to pet the dog, letting it lick his face while he petted it. He started up the steps, but stopped. He heard a noise coming from his bedroom.

Ruby, without heavy brogans to fumble with, had undressed before Ralph. She lay on her back in Franklin's narrow bed, her body chalk-white against the patterned quilt. Ralph glanced at her breasts, which had flattened and sagged to the sides. Her belly was less round and her hip bones more prominent. He liked her looks better when she was standing up, but he climbed on top of her. As the head of his penis pushed inside, he was for a moment afraid, as if a beagle had poked its nose under a rock-ledge after a possum and found a copperhead. But that feeling lasted only for a moment. If anything came to his mind, it was a cutting machine, the long prod gouging a seam of coal, its lurching power overriding the screaming teeth and black dust, the vibration tingling his cock down to its roots. And best of all, he could walk away after work. For Ruby, it was more like pulling tassels from an ear of corn, washing rhubarb, running her hands through the mattocked ground for potatoes. Ralph panted, snorting and grunting as his buttocks, like large white puffballs, rose and fell in the moonlight. He speeded up. Ruby lifted her legs and gripped his back, hunching upward. She was anxious that he would finish and leave her antsy. He gasped, lunged, and held himself convulsively in place, then sighed, collapsing on top of her. She gripped with the muscles of her pelvis, pressing and squeezing.

"Aow," he groaned. "It's awful tender when I come."

She sank limply under him. "That was pretty fast," she said.

"Wait a bit. You just wait a minute."

But she tensed suddenly and asked, "Do you hear that?"

"No," said Ralph. "I don't hear a thing."

"I do. Listen. We better get dressed."

Franklin was watching through the window. It was Ruby's legs he had seen lifted up, her white calves and feet in the air, her arms which had gripped Ralph's back. Franklin had undone the brass buttons on his overalls and pulled out his penis, his left knee trembling against the side of the house as he looked in, masturbating.

The back door opened and shut. Ruby heard Franklin's familiar shuffle in the kitchen. The light shifted in the bedroom; Franklin had moved the lamp and was opening and closing cabinet doors. She gestured to Ralph, mouthing *hurry up*, pulling him to the front porch before he had a chance to tuck his shirt in or tie his brogans.

"How come Gray didn't bark?" he asked in a whisper.

"It's his dog."

"Shit," Ralph muttered.

"You go on, now. Maybe I'll see you tomorrow evening at the hotel, after work."

Ralph tiptoed in his floppy shoes down the steps and disappeared into the weeds. Ruby needed to wash the perfume off her neck and brush the whiskey out of her mouth before Deborah and Keith got home, but she hesitated before going into the house. She wasn't afraid of Franklin, although in his dimwitted way he was oftentimes ill-humored. Every once in awhile a threatening look crept into his face, but he had a fit, then, and never hurt anybody but himself. She hardly ever gave him a thought. He was just there, about as real as a skillet, a scythe or a hoe. She sighed, leaned against the banister and looked at the dim mountain across the way. A sense of emptiness and self-betrayal pushed against her like a closing door. She stared blankly, her arms folded, and was oblivious of the night, which glowed as if the moon had cast pale phosphor down the hollow. Everything shone with a quiet, eerie whiteness. After a time she began to shiver. She sighed again, heavily, and went indoors.

Franklin towered in front of the kitchen cabinet, gnawing on cold corn bread and an onion, which he put aside as Ruby took up the tea kettle and basin. He watched her as she leaned to sponge her throat and face. She sat at the table to dry herself, glancing nervously at him, his bib overalls latched childishly high on his chest, his pant legs above his ankles, his shirt cuffs ending above his wrists, his stubble of beard and shaggy hair. She thought he was the most ridiculous, worst looking hick she'd ever seen. No wonder the out-of-state guests at the hotel made fun of men like him, calling them yokels, hillbillies, shitkickers. Slowly his posture began to change, though Ruby's agitated mind distorted his appearance. His neck seemed to angle forward. His head tilted back and his eyelids drooped sleepily, stupidly over his brown eyes. His lips parted and his tongue showed at the edge of his lower teeth. His arms hung loose at his sides. His chest rose, his abdomen hollowed and his pelvis arced forward and up. She shuddered. He looked like an ape that was hunching with an invisible woman. She glanced at him again. Abruptly, absurdly, his body appeared to be a nest, a honeycell of peace in which she could comfort herself. She could lean, place her head against his shoulder, her abdomen into the hollow beneath his ribs, and let the large sweet pleasure surge between her legs. She saw herself as she put her mouth to his.   The image was so horrible that she shouted, "You don't have to stare at me!"

"I seen you all," he whispered.

"How come you're back from church so early?"

"I runned home. I seen you all outside."

"Outside? You must be imagining haunts again."

"You was in my bed."

"You're all mixed up, Franklin. Nobody can be outside and inside, both."

"I seen you through the window."

"It's dark in your room, Franklin," she said. "A person can't see anything in the dark, especially what's not there."

"Moon's up. I seen you."

"You're always seeing something."

"Me and you can go in there," he whispered, stirring toward her. "We can do it."

"Don't be silly," she said, though she glanced at the bulge in his overalls and hated herself for doing so.

"We're not kin."

"You're my Granddaddy's son. You're my uncle, or half-uncle, at least."

"The old woman ain't my Mommy."

"Granny Deborah? Everybody knows that, but we're still related."

"You know who my Mommy is?" he asked, turning very pale.

"No," said Ruby. "It was long before my time."

"I don't know, neither. Don't care. Ain't the old woman. *Fuck.* Ain't Vida."

"Vida?" said Ruby, startled. "Why Vida?"

"She ain't. *Fuck fuck fuck fuck fuck.*"

"Franklin, you're going to have a fit!" Ruby screamed. "Quick! Get down on the floor like Granny says to do."

His body stiffened almost before he lay down. His arms trembled and shook at his sides; his rigid legs thrummed and beat against the floor, the heavy brogans clattering. Ruby, remembering Deborah's instructions, ran to put a pillow under his head. When the convulsions eased off, he breathed heavily through his clenched teeth, the saliva dribbling from the side of his mouth. He looked as if he were choking, so she knelt to loosen his collar button, turning her head away as she did so, avoiding the slobbery look on his face. She was so distracted that she didn't hear Keith and Deborah enter the house. Deborah, whose view of Franklin was blocked by the doorway, saw only Ruby kneeling on the kitchen floor. "What's the matter!" she cried out.

"It's Franklin! He's having a fit."

"Oh, him," said Deborah. "Get a washrag to clean up the spit. I'll get some blankets."

She hobbled into her bedroom. Keith, who had snuggled against her on the way from church, was puzzled by her ugly voice, but he forgot her instantly when he saw Franklin. To him, Franklin looked bigger lying on the kitchen floor than he did standing up, but he also looked like a baby. He looked silly, a big baby, as if he might crawl under the table or cling to the chairs. That wasn't right, not Franklin. He glanced at Franklin's face, heard his puffy breathing and saw the spittle on his chin, and that was enough. He backed against the wall.

"It's okay, honey," said Ruby. "Franklin can't help it. He won't hurt you."

"What's wrong?"

"He has epilepsy."

"What's that?"

"It's a disease, but he won't hurt nobody. It just looks scary."

"Will he wake up?"

"Your Great-granny will let him sleep on the floor. He'll be recovered in the morning."

"But who's going to sleep with me?" the boy cried out.

Deborah brought in the blankets, fretfully dropping them at Franklin's side. Ruby felt that her grandmother ought at least to show some consideration when the man was suffering. She looked reprovingly at her while spreading the blankets over him. "It's not his fault," she said. "He can't help it."

"He's not a fault but a reminder!"

"A reminder of what?"

"James! Your Grandpa James!"

"What happened, exactly?" asked Ruby, getting up. She was suddenly curious about her grandfather, how a man could be stupid enough to bring his bastard child in on his wife. She sat beside Deborah, who had slumped into a kitchen chair.

"It's so long ago, now, I ought to got over it," Deborah sighed. "But I ain't, and it's almost thirty years. I wasn't happy, then, what with the change of life and all. And anyhow, James was a ladies' man, always was, but reasonable till he come across a girl, Julie Beth Dickins, from Seng Creek. He just went wild, crossing the mountain ever night, and her only sixteen. Wasn't nothing I could do. What could any woman do when her breasts sag and her haunches shrivel up, and the girl as plump as a ripe peach. Crazy love. That's what it was. Crazy. I seen her at Barker's Store, carrot-haired and skin to put a baby to shame. And then one day he brings this infant home, saying the Dickins girl was pulling her hair out, screaming and crying because her family was against it. James said she was going to bury the baby in the weeds, so he took it. He brought it home. Oh, god! I could hardly bear up! I don't know what would have happened to the child if it hadn't been for Vida. She took him over, her fifteen and playing with him like he was a doll. When Vida married

46

and moved down the hollow, he runned down there ever day till Jake started rocking him home. Can you imagine that? A grown man throwing rocks at a child. Franklin was barely six years old. He's hardened his heart and ain't spoke to her for I don't know how long. You remember that about the sweetmilk and the buttermilk? He'd no more step through their gate than he would over a rock cliff. And with what little brains he's got, he's got enough to know nobody loves him. I know I sure don't, and never did. I'll be dead soon, and the Lord will never forgive me how I've treated him."

Ruby reached across the table and covered Deborah's hands with her own. "At least you kept him," she said. "There's not many women would do even that."

"All them years of rancor when the child's only fault was in being borned."

Keith approached the table, at a loss as to the particulars of Deborah's remarks. He wanted to hug her, and wanted her to hug him. "Is Franklin going to die, Great-granny?" he asked.

"No, darling. He'll be just fine in the morning."

"What is it, then? You ain't going to die, are you?"

"No, darling, but I fell washed out enough to."

Deborah hugged him close as he sobbed against her shoulder. Ruby turned red in the face, not knowing whether she was jealous or angry because her grandmother was doing for her son what was her own duty. But she was tired of caring. *Your man left you high and dry.* Ruby could still hear her mother's shrill voice. *And no more was he gone than the Japs bombed Pearl Harbor. He probably had a lot to do with it, the bohunk!* If William had left her high and dry, then it was the peak of a house she was clinging to after the flood, and Keith was a muddy rag doll in the window. She had climbed down, wrung the boy dry, brought him out of Hereford Creek and set him in the front yard of Leah's camp house. Then she turned and walked away, joining her kin—Charles and Della, Vida and Jake—and the others at the tavern at Ecco.

She glanced from her son to Franklin and her mind was confused for a moment. There was a man lying on the floor, as an infant does with its toys, though Franklin wasn't playing at anything, but more like a child who wore itself out and fell asleep among its play-pretties, right in the middle of the room for the cat to sniff at. And then there was a boy in his grandmother's arms, talking about death as if he were discussing seed corn. The situation should have been reversed. The child should have been on the floor, or better yet, in bed, and the man should have been talking about dying, or whatever, the way grownups do. And Deborah was giving all her love to Keith. What about Franklin? Ruby's heart went out to him for a moment. He was breathing laboriously, his lips fluttering against his teeth.

48

She watched Deborah stroking Keith's hair, heard him hiccupping into her shoulder, and figured to herself that she should have brought him to Deborah's in the first place, what with Leah off preaching half the time. But she got angry at having to come to Deborah's because, dammit, she lived too far up the hollow, miles from Ecco, and the place was so lonesome! And then she was angry with Keith, having to tug at him, as much as drag him, first to Leah's and directly afterwards to Deborah's. And shit, having to put up with Deborah's sad look when she left him bawling like a sick calf. She *had* to work. She was as good as single and *by god* she deserved to get a little fun out of life.

"Everybody's got to die some day," Deborah said to Keith as she stroked his hair. "But not now. Now you got to get in bed, the sandman's in your eyes."

"You working tomorrow, Mommy?" he asked.

"Yes, honey. I got to leave at daybreak."

Ruby took his hand and led him to the roll-away bed in Franklin's room. He shuffled away from it to tumble into the larger bed, but he was fully dressed and she stopped him. She tugged off his clothes and pulled down the quilt on the roll-away. He climbed in fretfully, and as she leaned to tuck him in and kiss his cheek, he turned away. She sighed, stroked his hair, and returned to the kitchen. She poured herself a cup of coffee, lit a cigarette and sat at the table with her grandmother. It seemed peculiar to be talking to her while Franklin was lying asleep on the floor right beside them.

"You reckon," asked Deborah, "that you'll find your man now the war's over?"

"Mommy don't know what she's talking about. We won't go to the FBI. If anything, we'll go to the Army recruiter in Riverton and they'll find him."

"And then?"

"I don't know. Maybe I'll get an allotment check."

"He won't come back to stay?" Deborah asked.

"No. He's got too high a plans. I don't know what for, but for sure not coal mining."

"Then you ought to go with him," said Deborah. "A woman's place is with her man."

"It's hard to know if he'll even show up. He might get a furlough or something."

"Well, I only saw him twice. He was a handsome man."

"Yep," said Ruby, "for whatever good it does anybody."

"God only knows what gets into them, unless it's jimsonweed or a young girl's smile. Did you know, Ruby, I had a man flirt with me, one time, right in my front yard."

"No! Who?"

"James's brother, Matthew, believe it or not. It was about the time Franklin come. Matt Waugh didn't think I was ugly."

"You're not ugly, Grandma. You never were."

"A woman like me's not ugly or pretty, just old. It was a long time ago. I wasn't tempted so much as I was flattered. He was a hero, you understand, come from the war in Europe, injured, younger than James by a long shot, and slender as a pole. He picked me daisies once, the silly thing, and I cried like I was thirteen. He had a mustache silkier than corn tassel. He played harmonica, too, sad as the skies in October. But he made over Franklin too much, and he died."

"Died? How?"

"Of the influenza. He'd gone way off, up to Wheeling."

"Why'd he go so far up north?" Ruby asked. "I wait table for the bigwigs come from up there."

"The steel mills? Who knows, except he was a man."

"I imagine you warmed to him some," said Ruby.

"He only come here to show off, and to aggravate James. Brothers are like that. Matthew weren't much older than my oldest who died over there."

Ruby sobered for a moment, and then said, "Matthew flirted with you a lot, I bet."

"Hush, girl!" Deborah chuckled. She was quiet for a while, then sighed and continued. "When I was young there was people, folks from all over, coming to this country like it was Canaan Land. They about turned the mountains around from wilderness, what with the pastures and tillage. But they sunk back into woods. The mines drew the men away from the fields, and there was strikes and

51

mine wars, especially in Boone and Mingo, and two of my sons killed in a slatefall. And now look. It's sucked ever one of you into Ecco and along the river. And into the beer joints, too."

"There ain't no harm in a little beer."

"I know, I know, and I sound like pucker-faced alum. It's time I got to bed."

The old woman moved stiffly around Franklin and into her bedroom. Ruby lit another cigarette, sipped at her coffee, and mused. So, her Granny once had a man come courting, just as she herself did now, if anybody could think of big-ass Ralph with a bouquet in his hands. And Granddaddy—even if he was a whoremonger—had stayed with her, which was more than Ruby could say for her man. She counted back six years, or almost six, since she was pregnant with Keith before the wedding. Only a year and a half, then William deserted her and Keith. He griped that she hung around her family too much and didn't look after Keith, yet the night he left he nearly beat the child senseless with a stick of stove wood. He was mean, like his father Ivan. *They do too stink.* That was her mother talking. *It's garlic, goat cheese, onions and I don't know what all. And Mary Brousek can't speak a word of English, much less read the Bible. They're all a bunch of foreigners, even if Ivan Brousek did grow the biggest tomatoes I ever saw.* Mean or not, William sure was a doll, blond-haired as a child, eyes paler than violets, and skin like a white rose. He was a man, sure enough, one of the strongest in the worst of Depression days. She remembered the mossy rock-ledge above the camp. She remembered the leaves and the sky all mixed in with the pleasure. And then him cursing the mines and worrying as union secretary over the books. He was gone soon afterwards, leaving her with a handful of company script, war coupons and a beat-up baby.

But she couldn't get over William. After him, all the men were bank-clothes in a washtub, her scrubbing out the coal dust, grime and grease, and all her loving was shriveled potatoes, mushy apples and blank milk. Those men made her forehead wrinkle as if she were hoeing in the hot sun; they made the mountains smothery and jungly. That was why she went to the tavern in Ecco, why she listened to Roy Acuff and Ernest Tubb on the peach-yellow Rockola jukebox, why she drank so much beer, why she went to bed with the likes of dumb-ass Ralph with the big dick. She sighed and butted her cigarette. Keith moaned on his cot and she trudged in to see about him. He was thrashing under the quilt. She grasped him by the shoulder, shaking him gently. "What's the matter, honey?" she asked. He jerked upward, wide-eyed and gasping. When he recognized his mother, he sighed and lay back.

"I was having a dream," he said.

"Did it scare you?"

"It sure did. There was chicken hawks circling around, and when they swooped to peck at me they didn't have no heads, just necks with blood dripping out. Their claws was in my shoulder, gouging me, and their necks was daubing my face with their blood. It was then I woked up."

"Lord, how awful!"

"Mommy, do you think they could get me?"

"Why, no, honey. I bet you dreamed that because you watched Franklin killing that chicken."

"You reckon?"

"Sure. You don't have to worry about no chicken hawks."

"Where do they go when they come down from circling?"

"They drop to—" but she stopped. She was about to tell him that the broad-winged hawks swooped down on quails, rabbits, chickens, whatever game they spied. In his dream he would have been such game. "I don't know, honey. Why don't you ask Franklin in the morning?"

"He'll be all right?"

"Sure he will. And listen, darling, I'm sorry I have to work, but you know we're living with Granny. We can't just mooch off her. I have to pay for the food we eat. You understand?"

"Yeah, I guess so," he said.

"Okay. Now, you go to sleep."

"Well. Night, Mommy."

Returning to the kitchen, Ruby filled the basin for a sponge bath. She wiped under her arms and squatted to wash between her legs. She did so near the door, behind Franklin. She tossed the water into the back yard and hung the basin on a nail. Before she blew out the light, she glanced at Franklin and was surprised by his face. Gone was the pinched brow, the squinted eyes, the tightness about his mouth, the obstinate stupidity of his face. His eyelashes were long and delicate, his eyebrows arched, his lips well-formed. He was actually handsome. She went into the living room, wound and set the Big Ben alarm clock. She turned the wick down in the kerosene lamp and blew into the bowl. In the bedroom, she undressed and took her nightgown out of the chifforobe, catching sight of herself in the mirror as she closed the door. Standing naked before the mirror, she saw her body in the glow of the bedroom lamp, saw her black curly hair, her breasts, smooth and firm, their whiteness shaded and highlighted. She caressed her oval, mounded belly. She gazed at the soft arcs of light on her breasts and plucked at her nipples. They hardened like the toasted tips of meringue.

Keith lay for a long while in the side room with the quilt wadded against his chest. He heard the hooing of an owl, the mice in the walls, the ticking of the alarm clock. He had to pee, though what with Franklin in the kitchen, the idea wasn't too terrifying. He scooted out of bed, and with the back door open, he stood at the edge of the porch and urinated into the yard, looking back at Franklin as he did so. He hurried inside and locked the door. Franklin was lying on his back, breathing quietly. Keith touched his cheek, picking at the dried spittle. Franklin stirred and turned on his side, his arm outstretched toward the boy. Keith snuggled against Franklin's chest, his head resting on the man's arm, and fell asleep.

Chapter 3

Vida strode out her back door into the dawn, a humming bustle of energy. She was twitchy as a squirrel, a bundle of slender muscle and lean sinew, and sleek at forty-three, with only the finest of crow's feet about her dark shiny eyes, her cheeks only slightly sunken about her false teeth. She took a large pail from the back porch and hustled into the pasture, heading for Betsy, though the heifer ought to be named swish-tail, the way she whipped it across the back of person's head and shoulders, as if she were trying to rid herself of the world's biggest fly. And she'd kick at the pail, too, and knock it over if she weren't watched out for. Vida entered the shed, grabbed the three-legged stool she got from Deborah's and settled herself beside Betsy. She liked the animal smell; it comforted her. She stroked Betsy's flank and spoke softer words to her than she ever did to her children. She settled the pail just away from her knees and went at it, squeezing and tugging the teats in rhythmic alternation. Warm, creamy milk streamed into the pail so forcefully that the bottom pinged with the force until it began to fill and foam, then the sound was a steady splash as the pail filled. Vida's mind worked as efficiently as her hands, and she was thinking it was a damned shame that Jake had to nigger-rig a shed that would hardly stand up, much less hold a horse, a milk cow and the feed bins. But Jake wasn't worthless. He was a good miner, a good provider, even if he did slop things around the house and drink too much, but age must be getting to him because he didn't want to do it in bed except maybe twice a month, and that wasn't enough for her. Not having it made her jittery and quarrelsome. She then thought of her mother's big barn at the head of the hollow and wished she could somehow transport it, complete, to stand where her shed did now. And thinking about the barn made her think of Matthew. Lord, how many years ago? Twenty-eight? The sweet thought of her Daddy's brother slowed her hands. Betsy balked and kicked. "Just a minute, dammit," said Vida, renewing her efforts. "I'm nearly done."

And back at the house, as she was straining the milk into half-gallon jars to chill in the refrigerator, she thought of him again, how Deborah wouldn't let him sleep in the house, claiming that the place was too small, and with him knowing the big room at the back of the house wasn't used any more, except to hold junk, since Leah and the boys had left, Leah married and the boys at a boarding house over in Raleigh County till the accident. Deborah carried Matthew a blanket and a pillow to the barn and set him up in the loft, frowning and warning him not to smoke. Vida hadn't thought much about the arrangement at the time, but over the years she realized that Daddy James and Deborah were worried that Matthew might try to seduce her. She also saw that the way Matthew played with Franklin was nothing but to coddle up to her, although he did seem to like the baby, cuddling and gawing over it like a fool. And at night, when the baby was asleep, she and Matthew played poker in the kitchen. It was a game she had only heard mentioned before, but she learned to play quick enough, taking more matchsticks from Matthew than he did from her, and him saying that was because he used his matches to light his pipe. They had to keep their voices down, since Deborah and Daddy James were in the living room, Deborah reading her Bible and Daddy James glaring at *The Farmer's Almanac.*

She carried the pail to the creek and rinsed it carefully, not wanting any mold or filth. She filled the bucket with creek water and carried it to the back porch, where she scooped cracked corn into a smaller pail, and then carried both to the chicken lot. After dumping the stale water and adding fresh, she spread the corn, coaxing the hens out of the chicken house, since they were touchy about a hand slipped under their breasts and would cluck and peck. The back of her hand had been bloodied more than once. She swung the bucket at the rooster that was approaching her menacingly, and while the hens were busy gorging themselves in the lot, she entered the cramped chicken house to gather eggs. The place had a molty, choking odor and she was glad to get away from it. Outside the lot, she sickled horseweed and stickweed, and as she was stooping she thought of her Daddy James, how often she had seen him lean to some task or another, and then stand ramrod straight, as if to bend were slavery or the like. She knew why he was so miserable the last years of his life. He was too stubborn or too prideful or too old to work in the mines, and he stood in his fields watching miners bring home and burn more money in a week than he could scrape together in six months. He had two sons dead in the mines. He hated mining and miners, and whenever he went to Ecco he walked stiff-backed and stiff-necked as a high priest in a whorehouse. He was barely polite to Jake, his own son-in-law. She threw the weeds into the chicken lot. Give them a few bugs to peck at instead of each other. She put the eggs in the refrigerator door. The little pockets provided for them, the small half-cups in the door, she had to admit, made her ridiculously happy.

She rinsed both pails again at the creek, dried the smaller one and took it to the strawberry patch, thinking that she would never grow strawberries again, not with having to chase among them like a scarecrow beating the kids out. It was bad enough slapping them across the head, keeping them away from the grapes and pulling them by the legs out of the apple tree, without keeping track of strawberries. And these were late ones, the last of them, none bigger than a thumbnail, and they were never quite sweet enough. That was also true of her Concord grapes; the skin was too thick, the seeds too large, and never enough pulp. The same with the apples, bountiful but ribby and worm-eaten. But she wanted her mother to have strawberries, so she picked them, thinking again of the past, of the old days, the time when Matthew simply disappeared, not a word for months, then a postcard of the Ohio River with the message, *I'm a steel man, now. Love, Matthew.* And then the news of his death, no funeral or nothing, just a telegram from somebody at Wheeling Zinc Company. He died of influenza and was buried quick. Vida's throat tightened. It seemed she could hear his harmonica playing, and her voice telling him to lay off the mournful tunes that would make the jowls of a hound dog drag the ground. Damn, she thought, here I'm going to weep in my strawberry patch. People would think I'm broken-hearted over the runty things. She gathered a pailful and returned to the house.

As with her fruit and vegetable garden, her house sprawled about profusely thin, with rooms nailed on, covered with tarpaper and batten boards; thin like her husband Jake, who was shamblingly tolerant of her bossiness; and her children, Beulah especially, grown and with kids of their own, all of whom wandered in and out of her house much as ants do at an anthill, seemingly at random and frequently bewildered. Her hens steadfastly laid small eggs, and Betsy her cow, profuse as she was, had a taste for wild onions. But there was always just more than enough.

"Wake up, sleepyhead!" she shouted to Josephine, who was staying over and asleep in one of the tacked-on bedrooms. "I'd hate to have you think you're visiting just so I could put you to work. You're better off here while Leah's in Boone County. I'm not asking much. Are you listening to me?"

"Huh?" mumbled Josephine, turning languidly onto her back. "Oh, Aunt Vida. What? I'm listening."

"I want you to keep your eye on the kids while I'm up at your Granny's. I already milked the cow and fed the chickens. Just fix the children some oatmeal and keep them from gouging each other's eyes out. And I've washed Pete's diapers. That child's too old for diapers, but I can't tell Beulah nothing, so they're washed. You hang them on the line when the sun gets higher. That's all I want you to do, you hear? I got to talk to Mommy about the Fourth."

"You go on," said Josephine. "I'll be up in a minute."

"I should be back before noon. Hang the diapers out, now."

"I'll be sure to."

If anything could get Josephine out of bed, it wouldn't be diapers but her cousin Danny so that she could parade in front of him in her cotton nightie. Danny was the only reason she came to her Aunt Vida's, anyway. He was fourteen years old, her first-cousin, skinny and smooth-limbed, and with hair already around his dick. She had seen it.

Vida sacked the milk and strawberries and headed up the hollow. Above the house she stopped for a look at Jake's horse, Fireball, which was a funny name, since he was gelded and didn't have any balls at all. He trotted up and stretched his long face over the barbed wire. She patted and stroked his neck, then hurried on, thinking of the grass, the oats and corn, which should be going to her cow. It was seldom that Jake rode the worthless old swayback, and he never took it out of the hollow. But the drunks loved rubbernecking when he rode into the yard, bigger than John Wayne, dismounting and tying Fireball to a fence post at the side of the house, and that was enough for Jake. Then Danny, cursing his Daddy, had to walk it back to the stall, and even he was too lazy to take the saddle off, and she ended up with the task, the same way she ended up watering and feeding both animals. Further up the road, along the narrow, rocky fields which also belonged to the family, she noticed the green nubs of blackberries beginning to swell on the vines. The road narrowed, and dawn seemed to darken a little. But as she made her way up the path to her mother's house, the sunlight broadened and sloped away on each side of the ridge, although the clearing, which had once been farmed, was now grown over in greenbriars, sumac and sassafras.

Vida looked up at her mother's house. But, in fact, it was Daddy James's. Though weathered to a soft gray and slightly atilt, it still dominated the slope, thrusting out from it, and treeless. *Don't want no damned trees in my yard. There's enough of them in the mountains.* She remembered him saying that. So, Deborah never got her weeping willows or her dogwoods. Vida saw her father as he was in the album, stiff-backed, his hands at his side, appearing somehow distant from Deborah, and much larger. And Vida thought of him like that, larger than life. *Daddy James.* The name itself had dark reverberations, like axes felling trees, like a sledgehammer against a chisel, splitting sandstone. He was certainly far away, now, dead for two years, but he had always seemed to Vida to be an old man, almost fifty when he brought Franklin home. And whatever anybody said, she believed that Matthew was the father of Franklin, not Daddy James. That had been her notion, her conviction, actually, for years. Matthew was up to screwing around, and Deborah had warned Vida off his kind. In fact, that's why Deborah made him sleep in the barn. A man like him was a lady-killer and after anything in skirts, including Vida's fifteen year old skirts, even if she was his niece. But hell, that was twenty-eight years ago, 1918 for Christ's sake, and most every man, anyhow, was a womanizing lout, including Jake if she didn't rein him back.

She paused at the fence, admiring the day lilies on each side of the gate. She liked what lasted and sprawled and took care of itself. And they had taken care of them-

64

selves, spreading effortlessly along the fence line, the tall blossoms making up in profusion—their fluted, flat-orange sameness—for what they lacked in delicacy. She drifted again to 1918, seeing herself, Matthew and Deborah as they planted irises, lilac bushes and forsythia. Her mother laughed and pishawed, giggled and tished the whole summer long, the three of them like kids with two hoops and a scooter. Vida had decided then and there she wanted a man like Matthew for a husband. She knew, settling for Jake, that a lot was missing in the way of style. But she muttered approvingly nonetheless and climbed on up the path.

"Mother, where you at!?" she yelled.

"We're on the back porch!" shouted Deborah.

"I've brought milk and some strawberries," she said as she rounded the house, "but the things are littler than thimbles."

"I'll bet they've got flavor, though," said Deborah as she got up from her chair. "Sprinkle some sugar and cream on them and they'll be delicious. We just picked some English peas. Sit down for a while."

"I'm making plans for the Fourth and it ought to be a big one," said Vida, "it being the first after the war and all."

Franklin made an odd gurgling noise in his throat and picked up the milk. Both Deborah and Vida watched guiltily as he slouched toward the springhouse. He stored the milk and walked to the barn. As he shambled through the wide doors, Vida thought distractedly that somebody

65

ought to trim his shaggy hair. Deborah sighed at the faded blue X on the back of his overalls, and at how the stitching seemed to fit between men's shoulder blades as a harness on a horse or mule. They were hitched to an invisible wagon which stopped at the graveside. What was that wagon, and what was in it when it stopped? Finally enough of everything, of Jesus in the world, finally some happiness, some peace and quiet? If so, it jarred through a rocky ford a long way back and splashed mud in her face. She had trudged alongside an animal by the name of James. He could never stop, that was his problem, never stop working or whoring, especially whoring. There was Franklin to show for that, a rotten fruit shoved under her nose. She might have forgiven James except for the living witness of his betrayal. Franklin, for twenty-eight years, was evidence of the idiocy of love. Oh, God! She nearly rose from her chair, pressing her hands to her face. She saw a driverless wagon heaped with fodder which spilt in the rutted, uneven road, and she herself was walking beside the wagon, the wind blowing chaff in her face, the empty wagon-bed stretching forever.

"I ain't good for nothing but trembling," she said faintly, dropping peas on the floor. "Look at these hands, like burl roots."

"You're all right," said Vida, "only stop trying to do so much. Do you need me to come help clean?"

"No, Vida. Ruby cleans real good."

"And we don't need no wood," Keith spoke up. "Me and Franklin is chopping it. How come Franklin went to the barn? We ain't done here."

"Forget it, Keith, you little pecker-head," said Vida, sitting in Franklin's chair. "You're too young to understand."

"I'm six years old, going on seven."

"That's what I'm talking about. You go play, and I don't mean play with yourself. Take some of them strawberries."

"You can go play, darling," said Deborah as she scooped berries into his cupped hands. His mouth watered at the sight of the bright red fruit.

Keith headed to the barn with his strawberries, thinking that his Great-aunt Vida was funny, her voice gravelly as rocks in a bucket. Around her he wanted to giggle and dance. His Great-granny Deborah, though, left him peacefully somber, as in the yard sometimes, when he gazed at nothing and forgot where he was altogether. He saw a woman, once, at twilight, standing beneath the great trees, in dark green shadows at the edge of the clearing. The lowest branches nearly touched her shoulders; those above were a pale, sunlit green, and the shrubs in the clearing brighter still. Her features were indistinct, without shape or outline, and blurred in the dusk. She was motionless, although she appeared to be stepping forward, and without lifting her arms or speaking, she beckoned to him. Awakening with a start, he had turned to look at the house and the barn, as if to reassure himself he were still in the world. He got lost in the clouds sometimes, too, in those like great white mountains, and those far above like rippled feathers.

When he entered the barn, standing in the huge bar of sunlight just beyond the doors, he couldn't see Franklin in the dimness beyond, but once out of the light he spotted him at the other end, sitting on a rusted washtub. Keith walked up to him, stretched out his hands and said, "Here, Franklin, you want one of my strawberries?" Franklin looked up, shouted *fuck!* and slapped Keith's hands, knocking the berries into the dust. Astonished, Keith looked down at the scarlet berries; his cheeks burned and tears sprang to his eyes. "What'd you do that for!" he cried out, turning away and running from the barn. The women saw him hurry past the woodpile to the front of the house, where he crawled under the steps.

"You trust Franklin with Keith?" asked Vida. "I mean, what with Ruby being gone all week."

"Franklin's fits are bad, but he ain't got rabies," answered Deborah. "Him and Keith get along real fine."

"God how mighty, I wasn't throwing off on him, Mother. You said yourself his mind was worse."

"It is some, but not dangerous."

"I don't guess you see much of Ruby when she *is* home," said Vida, changing the subject, "her hanging around Ecco half the night with Charles and them no-accounts. Leah! What a sister. Her crew's as bad as mine for all her preaching, and Josephine is lazier than cat

68

shit. Ruby's so hot she's smoking up the road. Mother, leave those pans alone. I'll carry them in the house."

"Ruby's problem is she's restless," said Deborah. "She ain't got a mean bone in her body. She's more like her daddy George than she is Leah. She's like a dandelion seed, the littlest wind carrying her here and there."

"It ain't the wind picking her up, Mother. But Keith, if he wasn't so shy, he could spend some time at my house. You'd think he was hatched under a cabbage leaf and raised by a scarecrow. Sally and Luke's at the house, now. He could play with them, but he's the exact opposite of his mother. Ruby'd die if she was alone half a hour."

"Ruby's had it rough," said Deborah.

"I know that, but she oughtn't leave Keith so much. She's just like Leah, who can never sit still, only what Ruby's after ain't God. I don't understand how anybody could leave their kids, like they do that bunch at my house."

"Like we done Franklin," Deborah remarked.

"Mother, you're bringing that up again. It's all in the past and you're dwelling on it too much. You ought to let old dogs lie."

"I know, I know," said Deborah, "but I can't help it. It's Keith. He casts my mind back."

"Well, Christ on high, I can't help it if Jake run Franklin home. That was twenty years ago, or more, and I was just married. My belly was bigger than a watermelon. And what man would take on a six-year-old moron, anyway?

69

Nobody would expect him to. Besides, you took good care of him when I left."

"No, I didn't."

"Hell, Mother, nobody'd expect you to love him like he was your own."

"Yes, they would," said Deborah.

"Who?"

"Jesus would."

"Shit, Mother. I mean somebody from around here. Come on, let's get these peas inside. I'll have Jake come and get you on the Fourth. Is one o'clock a good time?"

"That's fine," said Deborah. "Franklin won't come, but Keith will. Thank you for the berries, Vida, and the milk, and I want to give you some squash, if you'll help me gather them."

"Course I will. You know how much I love squash."

"I'll get a poke."

They took the peas indoors, and as they were walking toward the garden, Vida said, "It's funny how memories are, ain't it? I was thinking about Matthew, about the summer and how we planted the shrubs and—"

"James didn't like that none," said Deborah.

"Daddy James didn't like nothing," said Vida. "But the point is how the good gets mixed in with the bad, how we had so much fun with Matthew and then he died, how pretty Franklin was as a boy, especially how sweet he was, all quiet and somber-eyed, and then to find out he was retarded. He couldn't even go to school. Keith must be doing it to us, you know, casting our minds back, as you said."

Franklin came out of the barn. He trudged to the woodpile and squatted, hump-shouldered, tossing scattered pieces of stove wood onto the stack. Keith, hearing the women's voices and the racket Franklin was making, peered from the steps. The women were admiring the garden, Vida rattling on about the Fourth, how Deborah could bring her broccoli and cauliflower. There'd be fried chicken, hot dogs and hamburgers, slaw, macaroni and potato salad, deviled eggs, pickled eggs, dinner rolls—not biscuits but dinner rolls—cakes, pies, watermelon, ice cream, cases of pop and beer, probably whiskey, too, but she would just as soon not have it around because it made jackasses out of the men. She didn't want firecrackers, either, but the kids got hold of them somehow. The grownups could dance to the Victrola, since she was going to string up some lights for the evening.

Franklin stood up with the ax in his hand, and as he walked toward the women, he raised it upward. Keith thought for a second that he was lifting it onto his shoulders, since he usually carried it that way, but as he raised it above his head Keith screamed in his piercing child's voice, "Franklin!" Vida turned to see Franklin towering before her, tall and straight, disdainful, contemptuous. She wanted to scream, but all she could manage was a choked howl.

"Franklin!" screamed Deborah and Keith simultaneously, and Franklin paused, the ax high over his head, then let it drop behind him as he fell, rigid and convulsive at Vida's feet. She stared at him, dumbfounded and terrified, as the seizures racked his body. Deborah knelt before him to cradle his head and Keith came running from the porch steps. Gray appeared out of nowhere, leaping onto Franklin's chest and barking in his face.

"Get out of here, you god-damned dog!" Vida shouted.

The dog moved off a few feet but continued to bark. Keith whacked him with a piece of stove wood, which sent him howling under the house. Deborah turned Franklin's head to the side so that the spittle would drain. Vida, standing above them, was no longer terrified but outraged. "I thought you said the son-of-a-bitch was harmless! Bejesus Christ, maybe Jake is right. Maybe he belongs in the State Hospital, not up here where he could split a person's head open with an ax! Did you see it? Double-bitted and shiny enough to blind you. God almighty!"

"Just don't say nothing to Jake," said Deborah, looking up.

"Jake, hell! I ought to call the law and have him carried off, myself!"

"Don't do that," said Deborah. "It would kill him."

"And what do you think he just tried to do to me?"

"What have we done to him!" wailed Deborah. "What have we done to him?"

"Well, you never gave him epilepsy, and he sure as hell ain't mine or Matthew's."

"Matthew?" said Deborah. "Franklin's your Daddy's child. What's Matthew got to do with it?"

"Nothing, I guess," said Vida. "Shit, I don't know. All I know is I ain't coming up here but what I don't watch out for myself. And you and Keith are welcome at my house any time, but not him, not after today."

"Jake wouldn't let him come to the picnic, nohow," said Deborah. "And you know you can visit up here any time. We'll keep watch on Franklin."

"God," said Vida. "Nothing like having a maniac around to keep your nerves on edge. And to think I carried strawberries up here. I'm going home. You be ready on the Fourth, you and Ruby and Keith, but not him."

"You want your squash?" asked Deborah. "Keith will get it."

"Lord, no. I got to get down the road. Josephine probably let the kids go hungry and the diapers sour in the tub."

"I'm sorry, Vida. He hasn't never done nothing like that before."

"I know he ain't, Mother. He probably wouldn't have done it, anyhow, whether you all hollered at him or not. A fit would have taken him, first, like they always do. It's just that he looked so much like...."

"Like what?"

"Never mind. I got to go. And you be careful around him, Keith!"

"I will. Bye."

"Bye, you all. God!"

Vida, scurrying down the road, was blind to what gave her pleasure on the way up, including the honeysuckle, which the sun was warming into fragrance. Franklin's face kept appearing before her. It was arrogant, dictatorial, staring down his nose the way Daddy James used to. Franklin had raised his arms above his head, the ax glittering in the air. She shuddered, trying to get a grip on herself. Jesus! To think she actually believed that Franklin had belonged to Matthew! Yet Matthew showed up practically the same day as the baby, almost like playthings her Daddy James had picked up at the store, pretties to distract her from the boys hanging around the house. They were both so sweet. Franklin never cried, and Matthew would hold him, babytalk him, kiss him and snuggle him against his neck. And there Daddy James would be, standing in the doorway, a sneer on his face as he turned to stride off to the fields.

Vida stopped in the road and wailed. The past rushed forward to obliterate her twenty-two years with Jake. Her husband and her children were a fitful dream; the past was the reality. Matthew had been the only man and Franklin was their child. Matthew was hers, and out of her innocent, virginal girl-love was born, in her imagination, a child. Matthew and Franklin had filled her days with such intensely fantasized love that their presence lifted her home life out of misery. They had overcome the cold hostility of her mother and father's house. They had made a home despite the emptiness and the cruelty. Matthew was her husband in a gentle guise, and Franklin was the child-doll for whom responsibility was more than play, yet so like play that every hour, every day, was sweet. Then Matthew abandoned her in death. She clung to her imagined child as she dropped to her knees, but she bent forward, knowing that she held nothing in her arms. Pressing her hands to her face, she moaned and wept.

In that long-ago past, she had ignored the boys who came courting, and then the men who came courting. But at the marriageable age, at her majority, Deborah had repeatedly said to her: think of Jake, what a fine young man, so handsome, so steady to work. And Jake was handsome enough, hard-working enough, and persistent in his courting enough to turn any girl's head. So, she married him and left her child to Deborah and Daddy James. But she hated her Daddy James. She hated Jake. How could a man stone a child standing at his gate? She saw the boy, his arms covering his face, his shrill cries of panic and despair. She saw him turn away and stumble up the road. She drew herself up straight and said aloud, "God damn Jake and Daddy James, both! Ain't neither of them worth a shit. Turds. They'd wax a car with a Kotex." She got to her feet, dusted herself off, wiped her face with the hem of her dress, and walked on home.

Franklin was easing into a comatose sleep. Deborah sat on the grass beside him, weeping in a dry hacking manner. Keith was standing next to her. She tugged at his hand and he squatted, looking into her twisted face, whispering, "Don't cry, Great-granny. He's been doing that a lot, and he always wakes up." She pulled the boy into her lap, hugging him, reaching down the generations to feel his child's body against hers, knowing that, for any good it might do Franklin, she had come too late to Jesus, that the one in her lap should have been, twenty-eight years ago, Julie Beth Dickins' child, the infant whose only sin was in being carried into her presence, whose only crime was in persevering. She wept for him, the one lying on the ground, slobbery, his breath hissing laboriously through his teeth. And she wept for herself, whose stern judgment had no effect on the irremediable past.

Chapter 4

Vida didn't mind a little rain doing her garden good, but coming down in a deluge worried her, and all at once, too, because the creek might rise in a flash flood. She'd never seen water higher than the sandstone flats behind the house, but there was always a first time. She fretted as she changed Pete's diapers, a child old enough to climb an oak tree and still pooping in its drawers; his rearing was wrong, and she'd have to talk to Beulah about it, only not now, not after Ralph came splashing to the house, yelling about George getting killed. Vida just hoped that Leah wouldn't hold a revival over the corpse, pointing to her dead husband and screaming that this was the wages of sin, death was, almighty death who at this moment was carrying her dead husband's soul to hell—if he could get ahold of it, that is, since George was probably limper in death than he was in life, like a half-filled sack of potatoes—and there, Leah would say, is where we're all headed if we didn't heed Jesus.

Vida sighed and put Pete in the baby bed. He whined and beat on the bars with a rabbit-looking rattle he'd chewed the ears off of. She didn't want to think where the plastic went, and then wondered about the other kids, they were so quiet. She found them, sticks in their hands, smearing a skull and crossbones on her headboard with lightning bug guts. The skull glowed in the dim room with a yellow leer. She screamed. "Sally! Luke! Get out of my bedroom! I'll pinch your asses off and see if you glow in the dark. You should be ashamed. Them little bugs never hurt a soul. They don't even bite or sting, and they twinkle like stars in the trees. Shame on you." The two kids scrambled around her with their jar of fireflies and headed for the back porch. She went to the kitchen for the wash-rag, and as she cleaned the headboard she made an effort to remember what her sister was like before she married George and before God struck, how bossy she was as the older one, and how she sucked up to Daddy James and sided with him against her and Deborah, as when his boots weren't cleaned and she blamed Vida, knowing full well it was her turn to scrape the mud and horse shit off and to lay on the saddlesoap, or when she simpered and coyed-up as she handed him his clean white handkerchief and tie of a Sunday morning and then smirked at Vida, or when she looked reprovingly at her own mother if the food came to the table thirty seconds late. She was Daddy James's girl, and in Vida's opinion, when George didn't fit the bill Daddy James drew up, she turned to God as the one who did. Vida was glad when Leah married. It permitted her some freedom, and then Matthew and all the years afterwards with Franklin, because Franklin and caring for him gave her independence from Deborah and Daddy James in their own house. Matthew. That was the comeuppance of a lifetime. She shuddered at the thought of herself on her knees in the middle of the road, screaming like a banshee for what never was in the first place, a silly dream that belonged to a teenage girl. Idiots and fools is what people were. For Leah, George was a pushover, the same as Daddy James, and they both dressed nice when they weren't at work, you could say that about them, if nothing else. The only thing was that George, when he was pushed, didn't spring back. He kept bending and bending till there was nothing left but to scrape him off the floor, whereas Daddy James snapped upright like the hammer of a .38 Smith & Wesson and would explode in a person's face. It had happened to Vida herself. She'd be deaf for three days after he boxed her on the ears, thunderstruck, powder-burned, and left with the knowledge that some souls in this world would as soon strike lightning in your face as to look at you. But he never hit Leah.

Vida hated her Daddy James, and after a lifetime of consideration she knew why. She didn't matter to him.

Leah might have mattered, but Vida herself didn't. She was as much as the nail he hung his horse bridle on, a plank in a stall, a feather of a barn owl, for all he cared. She was nothing to him, but Franklin became everything to her. She practically snatched the infant out of his arms, lavishing on the child the tenderness which should have been hers from Daddy James. But her hatred had leveled itself and was now a commonplace fact, like her false teeth and her thinning hair. She knew she loved Deborah, of course, but gave it no more thought than breathing, the same way she did Jake, except that Jake was going silent on her lately, not mean or anything like that—no man would be mean to her after Daddy James—Jake was just non-talkative but to the bottle he had too often under his nose.

She grabbed a basin, and in her bedroom took a whore's bath as she called it, splashing under her arms, between her legs and a quick swipe at her feet, and patting herself dry. She climbed into a clean dress, hoping that Jake had foresight enough to bring Della or Josephine to watch the kids. She slapped on some talcum powder, and in the living room drank at her cold coffee and lit a cigarette. She had made a mistake, mentioning to Jake about Franklin with the ax. Of course, she immediately began to lie. She told him Franklin was harmless; everybody knew that. Anything resembling stress sent him into a fit, and besides, he was raising the ax to a block of wood. That was the lie she told to Jake, to keep peace in the family. And it was true that the ax didn't bother her as much as what she saw in Franklin's face. She had seen her Daddy James's face, not Matthew's. Maybe, a few years ago, Jake would have sloughed it off. He would have shrugged and turned away, as he did with anything that would have caused him to have to think or do, but with her telling about the ax his face hardened. He almost scared her for a moment, the way his neck knotted and his hands curled into fists, the way he got red-faced and the filth spewed out of his mouth.

Jake's headlights lit up the road, so she grabbed her umbrella and went to the porch. Della sopped through the yard, and Vida, with a word of caution about the hellions in the house, hurried out to the car.

Leah's George getting killed, at least to Jake's way of thinking as he drove his wife and sister-in-law up the hollow—and in the dark and rain to boot—was nothing but a pain in the ass. Vida and Leah were worse than a terrier and a feist, though Jake had seen better looking feists, skinned, than Leah with a poke over her head. To Jake's mind, Vida was all right, not ending up biscuit dough like most women, and never pecking at a man's dick the way he figured sanctimonious Leah had done George's. Vida might be bony as a wet cat, Jake thought, but what she lacked in meat she made up for in action; her pussy was like a calf's mouth. She could wear a man out, wear him down to the nub, but at the moment his thoughts were on that old lady, Deborah, acting like Esther and Ruth in the Bible, all rolled up into one, always polite but never friendly, as if he came from those trashy people living around Ecco, which was where he did come from. But that was not it, exactly. She was never that friendly to George, either, and she did let Jake use the field across from his house for a horse pasture. Well, a cow pasture, too, but Betsy didn't count. Jake was glad that old man James had died. The thought of him dead stirred his spirits and blocked out for a moment the nearness of George's death.

"Damn, Jake!" complained Vida. "Don't drive so fast. These chuck holes will knock your kidneys out."

"Fast? I ain't doing all of five."

"Well, slow down anyhow. Now, Leah, tell us again what happened. Start at the beginning. I never did get it straight."

"Like I was saying, I had got off the train this afternoon from Boone County." She distracted herself immediately, as if to keep her mind off her dead husband. "I can tell you there's whole churches over there that needs redeeming as much as the reprobates and the backsliders do, but there was some good services in the revivals—the gathering at the altar, feet washing, praying and shouting, testimonials, singing and speaking in tongues. Lots of sinners saved."

"Any healing and snake handling?" asked Jake.

"We ain't like some apostolics I know of," Leah answered in a huff. "God didn't mean for us to handle snakes, but we could in the same way we could move mountains, and Jesus never called on me to heal the sick except by praying, in the same way He never called on you but to serve Him."

"We know all that," said Vida impatiently, "but what happened when you got home?"

"George weren't there, and of course I knew where to look for him. At the Ecco Pool Hall. He'd been drinking since noon, so I left him and went back to the house. About seven, Ralph and them heathenish children of ours come tearing in at the door saying George got run over by a train. The engineer was dropping cars at the siding and didn't see George on the tracks. He was sitting there."

"In the rain?" asked Jake.

"I reckon," Leah answered.

"Shit!" exploded Vida. "I'll bet it's the same son-of-a-bitch that's already killed two people on them tracks. He'd run his own mother down."

"May be," said Leah, "but there ain't no need in cursing. Anyhow, the ambulance took George before I hardly had a chance to look at him. We need to talk to Mother about the service. I want to bury George up there with Daddy James and the others."

It was Jake's impression that Leah was taking things mighty cool, and what the service meant was that, for the next three days, he had to walk on tiptoe as if through a roomful of dozing cats; he had to bow his head and act hangdog; he had to look at relatives with a sick smile and a shake of his head; he had to talk about George and the old days, or just yesterday, but not so much that George's family went hysterical. He liked having the two days off and helping to dig the grave, swigging at the bottle, or running for smelling salts or flowers at the Riverton florist, or pallbearing, anything other than pretending to grieve for a man who for twenty-two years was nothing more than a fence post that Leah and Vida strung barbed wire on, stringing it from George to himself, as they stood on opposite sides. Jake had no complaints against George himself, other than the fact that he married that Bible-pounding, shrieking-voiced Leah.

"George was fifty, wasn't he?" Jake asked.

"He'd of been fifty-one come September," Leah answered.

"It's raining cats and dogs," commented Vida. "Hope the creek don't get too high. Thank god we're about there. Do you think Mother will take the news and not faint? She's getting old."

"Yeah, she'll take it okay," said Jake. "She's been through a lot of deaths. We're getting to the age where all of us have."

"Shit, Jake," said Vida. "You're only forty-six. Being born in 1900 was lucky."

"I can't get close to the house," he said. "You all have to use the umbrella."

* * * * * * * *

Deborah, with the lamp at her elbow, was sitting on the couch, reading from the New Testament as best she could with her blurry eyes. Keith was curled up beside her, drowsily watching the pink flowers in the wallpaper suddenly fade and brighten as the light flickered in the draft. Franklin was sitting in the chair across. *Consider the lilies of the field, how they grow; they toil not, neither do they spin: and yet I say unto you, that even Solomon in all his glory was not arrayed like one of these.* There, now, Keith. That means you don't need nothing but spirit to follow Jesus."

"Solomon? Who was that?"

"A great king of Israel."

"What's *arrayed* mean?"

"His clothes, his robe and crown."

"Oh."

Franklin listened with interest despite himself. *Lilies?* He knew what tiger lilies were. *A great king?* That meant nothing to him but God, whatever He was besides the cause of Deborah's fits in church, and he was thankful for them, since they made her like he was.   He watched Deborah's fingers trace across the page; he listened to her words.   Why hadn't she ever read to him from the Bible? In all the years past, she had sat silent, her lips moving silently, and she never looked up, never noticed him as she went through the book.   He had, a couple of times, sneaked and opened the Bible, but the tiny black marks were as mysterious as those on the cans and jars were—*Clabber Girl, Karo, Bon Ami, Martha White, When It Rains It Pours*—except that the cans and jars he had figured out the use of, if not the meaning of the words.   He looked at Keith snuggled against Deborah's side, and instead of being angry, he had a thickness in his chest and throat, a tightness about his lips and eyes, and his vision blurred.   He had an urge to hold Keith.   But then he felt the handle of the doublebladed ax in his palm; he saw the bright blade as he raised it in front of himself.   An emotion akin to shame filled his mind.   He turned away.

"I see lights," he said.

"And there goes Gray barking his fool head off," said Deborah.   "We better see who it is."

They went to the porch and watched two figures, with a glare of headlights behind them, struggle up the path.   As the umbrella swayed about in the wind, it looked to Keith like one of the chicken hawks in his dream, a broad-winged hawk, swerving in the dark.   "Here, Gray!" Franklin hurried to the yard to restrain the dog.   The figures became less eerie as they approached. The headlights illuminated the mist in gray, ghost-like shafts which the two women walked out of. "Who is it?" called Deborah. The lights went out, and they heard a car door slam.

"It's us, Mother, me and Leah!" shouted Vida. "Jake's coming."

"Come in before you get drenched. What's the matter?"

"It's George," said Leah as they made their way up the steps. "He was killed this evening."

"George! He ain't on the swing shift."

"No. It was a train at Ecco."

"Oh, Lord! You all come on in. Franklin, start a fire for coffee!"

By the time they had settled in the living room, Jake came in. He chose a corner chair, expecting to be bored with a repeat of the tale, the patting and hugging and snotting, the funeral plans which they already knew, since George wasn't the first dead man they ever buried. He was soured by the thought of digging a grave in the mud. He slouched and lit a cigarette, thinking ahead to the food and especially the pints to be handed around on George's back porch during the wake. He hardly listened to the women until Deborah brought him up short.

"George as good as killed hisself," she said. "He always was a weak man. He had that sick look in his eyes, like a hurt dog."

"Mother!" exclaimed Vida, genuinely shocked. "You're throwing off on a dead man, and your son-in-law at that."

"I'm tired of not judging a man just because he's dead—"

"He was drunk," broke in Leah.

"Don't make no difference," said Deborah. "It started long before the bottle. He was weak and he raised weak children."

Leah glared at her mother. "Them's my children, too!" she shouted.

Vida could see that it wasn't Leah's purpose to admit that she had weak children, though Deborah clearly had a point. Charles, Leah's oldest, drank too much. The only hope was that Della, his wife, would straighten him out. She was a church woman, though Vida had to admit that it didn't keep her out of the Pool Hall. And Ruby! Vida didn't like to think of the word *floozy*, but her niece spent more time in the taverns than was good for any woman's reputation. And if Josephine had her way, she'd be right there beside her.

Vida was so stunned by her mother's outburst that she came to her sister's defense, which was some kind of miracle. "Hers ain't that different from mine," she blurted out. "Ain't nothing wrong with our kids. Well, Beulah, maybe."

Vida didn't have any children at home except Danny, her fourteen year old. The others came by to visit and to drop their children off—Sally and Luke—like hampers of soiled clothes. Beulah was doing it with Pete, only she was leaving him longer and longer each time.

Deborah shouted, "I let one man slip into death before I could give him a piece of my mind! Your Daddy James, hah! Look at the trash he carried home, a sick baby he tried to call an orphan, when any fool could see that the thing was his. And look what it's become, Franklin in yonder." She stopped abruptly and cried out. "Lord God! I'm picking on poor old George because of James!"

Leah couldn't help coming to her father's defense. "I don't want you throwing off on Daddy James!" she said. "He was a good man and a good father. If it wasn't for him we'd never of got through the Depression."

"You were his favorite," said Deborah. "How could you see he was weak?"

"He was a cruel-hearted son-of-a-bitch!" said Vida.

"He was not!" Leah shouted. "He was strong. He had to be. Look how he worked in the fields when the mines was down, how he provided for us, and with me and Vida already married and kids at the table."

"Wasn't no need," Jake spoke up for the first time. "We made do."

"He worked to hide from life," said Deborah.

"And what's that supposed to mean?" Leah snapped.

"To hide from me, from Franklin. He was cold and cruel, and behind that was emptiness. He was dead twenty years before he died."

"If he stopped feeling anything," said Leah, "it was because of his two sons killed in the mines. We all suffered for those brothers of ours, and now George."

"Oh, I'm sorry, I'm sorry," said Deborah, tears welling in her eyes. "My mind's been wandering of late. I keep drifting back to the old days. George, he was a sweet-tempered man."

Franklin removed a stove lid and set the percolator directly over the fire. The people in the other room would want their coffee quick. He set out cups, spoons and sugar, and went to the pantry for the canned milk. An image kept flashing in his mind: Jake standing at the gate, swearing at him, *You little bastard, you get your ass back up the road, let that high-toned Christian up there live with your shit, and James, too, thinking he's better than us, and him dragging a whore's offspring up there to start with! Bastard!* Behind Jake he saw Vida, who was wringing her hands and squirming, her mouth open in some kind of wail. Franklin's head began to ring. He began to see that it was Jake he hated as well as Vida, maybe more than Vida. He concentrated on the water bubbling up in the glass bulb in the lid, watching it turn brown. He scooted the pot over and replaced the lid. "Tell them it's ready," he said to Keith as he headed out the back door. It was Jake he wanted to get away from, the man he wished was dead like Daddy James was, Daddy James who fell back in the field with a heart attack, in a fit that killed him.

"George's children loved him, and I loved him," said Leah in the appropriate funereal tone.

"Well," said Vida, who didn't want to see a quarrel between her mother and her sister, but who wasn't averse to taking things on herself. "Him and the kids would have had it easier if you'd stayed home more."

"He was loved enough."

"By who? You were traipsing around preaching."

"I have a duty to God," said Leah. "I was called."

"Crap. It was George you was hearing who called, most likely."

"Are you telling me I was a bad wife and a bad mother?"

"Shit, Leah. He must have had it rough keeping the house and working, too."

"I wasn't gone three hundred and sixty-five days a year."

"You was gone enough," said Vida.

"You two stop it, now," said Deborah. "Hissing like snakes."

Keith, standing in the doorway, knew what snakes were like. He had seen two of them in the road, a copperhead and a blacksnake coiled about one another, hissing and biting as they writhed. He had watched, fascinated, until Franklin came running and killed them both with a hoe.

"Maybe if you'd stayed home," Vida shouted, "there wouldn't be Keith harassing Mother! You got a grandchild but no son-in-law, and now the boy's yoked around Mother's neck."

"Keith ain't no bother," said Deborah. "He's my angel, my Great-grandbaby."

Keith smelled smoke as the stovepipe whined in the drafts of wind. He understood only vaguely what was being said. But he knew there was trouble, and it was more than the wind in the chimney, the kind of wind, Franklin said, that burned the creosote in the pipes and might burn the house down, too. Keith knew who George was, the sad-smiley man at his Granny Leah's, though he couldn't make any real connection between the man and Leah herself, the man who said maybe two words to him and once laid his hard, callused hand on his head as soft as a feather. George was his mommy's father, his grandfather. Ruby had told him. Keith could see George laid out in halves. *Cut him right in two*, he had heard Vida say on the porch.

Vida opened her mouth and closed it. She realized that she was about to accuse her sister of driving George not only to drink but to suicide.

"I was gone, huh!" shouted Leah. "What was there to be gone from?"

"From George and your children, your duties to them."

"Mother thinks he was sweet!" Leah squawked, forgetting altogether that Jake was in the room. "You think he was put upon! But let me tell you, he wasn't no man, and he hadn't been for years!"

"You mean he didn't take you to bed?" asked Vida, so astonished that she forgot to quarrel.

"That's right. He quit when Josephine was about two."

"Fourteen years ago!?"

"Around there, yes."

"I'll be a witch's tit," breathed Vida. "It's a miracle you didn't turn to God long before you did."

"Jesus was my rescue."

"Well," said Vida. "No fucking wonder."

"Vida!" said Deborah. "Don't blaspheme."

"Shit, Mother, it's like a brick just fell on my head. Why didn't you say something before now, Leah?"

"We didn't talk, not after we was married with kids, anyhow."

"Jesus. We ought to have."

"Maybe so," Leah sighed. "But we didn't. It's water under the bridge, and I'm as much to blame as anybody."

Jake shivered at the trickle of sweat running down his side. He shifted in his seat, and his hand trembled as he pulled another cigarette out of his pack. He could see George standing in front of the women, naked, with his hands tied behind his back and his feet bound, them flailing him with a horsewhip, except it wasn't his flesh they were after but his character, or whatever it was stayed on when a man died, his reputation, some respect left over, even if he was a spineless slug, some decent word and not a Judgment Day by females whose only concern for a man was his paycheck and his hard cock.

"George," Leah went on in such a state of distracted relief that she was practically in giggles. "He'd get way down and wouldn't move a muscle other than getting to work and the beer joints. He'd sit in a chair so long I'd just sweep around him."

"All I ever thought was he was quiet," said Vida.

"Yep, quieter than a tomb, and dull as a mildewed closet. He'd never take me nowhere."

"He didn't talk much when we was all sitting around drinking, either."

"He wasn't mean or nothing," said Leah. "He just wasn't there."

"He provided," said Jake defensively.

"So does a field of potatoes," Leah shot back.

"Well, he's dead now," said Vida, wanting no trouble between her husband and her sister. Trouble between herself and Leah didn't matter.

"Deader than a doorknob," Leah cackled, choking on her sobs and laughter. "Deader than Grant's tomb. He was run over and squashed, and soppier than a wet dog."

94

"Here, that's enough," said Deborah. "You all get some coffee."

The two sisters went to the kitchen. Jake heard a clatter of cups and spoons, and Leah mumbling about how peculiar Franklin was acting, more peculiar than usual, but she really meant that Franklin wasn't handy to open the can of condensed milk. She had to hunt for the opener. Peculiar. That was the truth if Jake ever heard it. He waited—listening in on their conversation—for Vida to tell the story about Franklin trying to ax her to death, but she changed the subject to George, how Leah ought not to have stayed with the no-dick bastard for fourteen years, and how come she never left him flat-ass for a man worth cooking for? Huh, Jake grunted. As if a man had to pay for his food with a hard-on when he'd already paid for it in the mines forty hours a week. He shifted angrily in his chair, thinking that marrying into the Waugh family might have been a mistake. Old man James had been worse than Custer, and Deborah must think she was God's mouth Itself, and between the two was Franklin, a lunatic ax murderer, or almost anyway, as Jake had pieced Vida's story together.

Through his self-righteous anger, only the faintest tic of guilt twitched at Jake's face. In his mind was an image of Franklin in front of the new-built house, the boy standing there blubbering and blowing snot, of him being pushed on the shoulder, turned around and shoved through the gate, of him lingering in the road till Jake threw rocks and forced him back to Deborah's house. It wasn't Jake's place to take his father-in-law's bad blood. He told Vida twenty-two years ago, before they got married, that no bastard was coming with the bride. It wasn't his fault that Vida took care of the idiot like a mother would. He glanced at Keith standing in the doorway and thought that there was another one, not exactly a bastard, but the closest anybody could come to it what with Ruby having been deserted by her husband so fast, and to top it off the damned kid living with Deborah like Franklin had been for twenty-eight years. He glanced at Deborah and saw her staring at him. He was acutely uncomfortable, and was glad when the women brought the coffee in.

"It's still raining piss out of a boot," said Vida, handing Jake his cup.

"We should be going pretty soon," he said. "The road'll be getting bad."

"Mother," said Leah. "I want to bury George up here."

"I'd expect you to," said Deborah. "It's the family grounds. Poor George. His children sure did love him, Charles and Ruby when they were small."

"That's true," said Leah. "He never stopped them as kids from crawling on his lap. He was kind to them, and easygoing, even with Josephine."

"I never saw him take a belt to one," said Vida.

"He was a hard worker, I know that for sure," Jake chimed in heavily.

The calming litany swept over Keith and he stumbled to the couch and his great-grandmother. He snuggled sleepily beside her. The meanings didn't matter, only the easing off of trouble; the lulling and surging lamentation calmed him. It was led by Deborah, whose praises of George were blurred by her choked voice and piercing cries. She was spontaneous as a child. Keith gripped her arm, suddenly awake and weeping in the generality of sorrow and helplessness.

Franklin, outside the house and stooping under the living room window, rejoiced in the sorrow led by Deborah, but something again made his chest tighten; the sound made his eyes tear over. He listened and listened, and above the other weeping he heard Keith's high, piping cries. They didn't mean anything. Keith didn't know what he was sobbing about, even Franklin could understand that. But Franklin didn't know why his fits came on. He didn't know why Vida had left and wouldn't take him. He didn't know why he hated Deborah but didn't want to. He shuddered in the cold rain. His shirt and overalls were drenched. He wiped the rain off his face and went to the barn where he could watch as the car pulled away.

Jake, for a moment or two, was at a loss, as if he had awakened from a whiskey nap and didn't know where he was, what the hour was or the day of the week, or if he were at home or at some strange place. He struggled to determine what was going on. Then he recognized the commotion, which reminded him of howling dogs when the train coupled cars at the tipple, or when kittens meowed and clawed at the burlap sack they were stuffed into for drowning—rackety sounds, *oh lord and our deliverance* and *oh he was a sweet man, a kind man* and *death catches us unawares* and *poor children*—a caterwauling of teething babies and weaning pups, of whining and blubbering and bawling. The noises aggravated him. They made him uncomfortable and sweaty, and when they subsided he turned to Vida.

"I think we'd better go," he said. "The rain's let up some."

"I reckon we should," she said, sniffling and wiping her eyes.

They made ready to go, rising and tugging at their clothes. They carried their cups to the kitchen. Vida and Leah tucked their hankies in their purses; Vida took up her umbrella. They murmured good-byes and blurted out last-minute instructions: George's people to call, the miners' burial fund, the preacher, the headstone. Jake helped the women down the path. As he opened the door for them, he looked up at the house and saw the two, Deborah and Keith, standing on the porch, dimly silhouetted by the light through the screen door. He wondered where Franklin was. Probably out slaughtering Fireball and Betsy with an ax.

After the bumpy drive on the muddy road, Vida ran inside and Della hurried to the car. Jake drove her and Leah home, refusing Leah's invitation to come in when he got there. He saw no reason for visiting now, since he hardly ever did when George was alive. Anyway, he had a fifth stashed on the back porch, and he needed a drink. When he got home he was bothered by Vida's silence, because she seldom was. She only remarked, "You belabored them chuck holes. Leah must have thought you didn't want to drive her home." *No shit* was what he wanted to say, but he kept silent. The whole evening upset him. For years she had asked him to take her side against the Dingesses, but tonight it seemed like she switched on him, or whatever, and it pissed him off.

"Why don't Leah keep Keith?" he asked. "She's his grandmother, not Deborah."

"She's gone off preaching too much. You know that."

"That preaching's a crock of shit."

"Not nearly as big a one as her life with George," said Vida. "I've know women do worse in her situation. You see them in beer joints all up and down the river."

"May be," he mumbled.

Vida checked on the grandkids, feeling for wet sheets or if they'd gone to bed with their clothes on. It occurred to her that Jake was criticizing her for keeping the grandchildren, though it was just in a pinch that she was doing so. It was true that Ruby and Keith wouldn't stay at Leah's. Why would they want to, anyway, what with Leah nagging them half to death, and preaching till they wished they'd never heard the name of Jesus Christ. When she was home, that is. And what was wrong with Jake, anyhow? He acted like he had the heebie-jeebies, and not just because of George but because, well, she didn't know just what. She'd worry about it later. Everybody's nerves got frazzled when there was a death.

Jake took his bottle out of its hiding place and trudged to the kitchen. He took down glasses, poured whiskey and water, and sighed, relaxing for the first time all day as he chased the fiery whiskey with a drink of water. Poor dumb-fuck George, he thought as he sat at the kitchen table, it was a train got him sure enough. It was Leah's Glory Train, and he bet a hundred dollars it was *her* held off on him. Probably slept with a ladling spoon between her legs, or a skillet most likely, if her twat was anything like her mouth. To hell with her. And George, too. Jake didn't want to think about it.

He thought, rather, of the burden laid upon men's shoulders, of the load they suffered under, and how both hands were busy, one reaching out to push the branches aside, the other reaching back to pull the wife and children through. He sighed, lit a cigarette, and drank. Life was hard, damned hard, and unfair, too, if the hand reaching back got spit on, got slapped and pushed away. He shivered suddenly and sweated, aware that his own hands were peculiar, that the bottle and the two glasses—the table itself and the chairs, the stove and refrigerator, the wallpaper—everything seemed fake, like the store fronts and the store dummies at Ecco. "Jesus Christ," he mumbled, trembling as he poured himself another drink.

Vida was in bed but couldn't sleep. She was thinking about Jake, him getting drunk out in the kitchen. He would stagger into bed after awhile, smelling like a sour polecat, and he would wake up in the morning, ranker than when he went to bed, and grouchier than a baby with the rash. If she could have wished the evening different, she wouldn't have had him present during the quarrel at Deborah's, because there's some things women say together that men oughtn't hear, in the same way she wouldn't want to hear what men said at the mines, when they called a spineless fellow a pussy, or one they were disgusted with a cunt, or when they talked about a woman as if she were a slab of bacon at Barker's Store. She had overheard such talk right in her front yard, when miners loafed with Jake before going home or to the midnight shift of a Sunday. When she first heard their nasty mouths, she sloughed it off as talk about women with herself being the exception, that she wasn't a woman, somehow, until one time she heard a younger one say to Jake that she, Vida, must really do a job on his dick, since she used her hands on

Betsy, and they must be stronger than a sump pump. Jake jumped the younger one's ass, telling him in a shouting voice that it was all right to talk about whores but not his wife, or any of the miners' wives, miners who were good men, fine workers, and their women were decent and not to be blabbed about like they were sluts. Of course she knew what Jake was talking about, and in a twisted way felt sorry for the younger man, who hadn't learned his manners as to which woman to disparage and which not, and she was pleased, too, that Jake came to her defense, though the hand-job remark probably did piss him off because she'd used it on him a lot, lately, so she could arouse some interest on his part and climb on top. The thought suddenly occurred to her that maybe Jake was wearing out, that he was surly and grumpy because of it, and afraid not just because he wasn't getting it up like he used to, but because of dying. It was difficult for her to think of Jake as afraid and unhappy, but it must be so, or a situation very much like it, and she decided to go easier on him, not to ask for so much.

Then her Daddy James came to mind, and she wondered if a similar thing had happened to him, that he got desperate and afraid, that even looking at Deborah and her change of life reminded him of dying, and his sons killed in the mine, so he ran off to Julie Beth Dickins, a woman who could stave off death. Vida's heart thawed in pity for a moment, but then hardened in anger. Asshole men. Didn't they know they had to die like everything else in the world? And look what staving off did for Daddy James. He got a moron out of it. Poor Franklin. Tears welled in her eyes but she blinked them away. She blinked Franklin out of her mind and settled on George. She wasn't embarrassed, exactly, by the open display of grief for him at Deborah's. Deborah was simple enough, old-fashioned enough to wail and carry on in public without a blush of a second thought. People nowadays didn't act that way. They hid their suffering, or maybe they didn't suffer like people used to. Anyway, Vida felt kind of ashamed for crying openly, in the way she would feel about changing her underwear in public. But she had to admit that it did feel good, crying aloud like that, as if she were a child again, broken-hearted and weeping as if the whole world were lost.

Well, George was lost to the world, and she thought that maybe he had an inkling of what was happening to Daddy James years back, and what was happening to Jake right now, and figured he wanted no part of the fear and unhappiness. He gave it up for peace. And he was a peaceable man. He had a calming effect, especially on kids, the way he laid his arm across their shoulders, patted their heads, listened to them as if he had forever to do it in. He could calm a party, too. He could bore it to death. But that sort of calm would never sit with Leah, not that Vida blamed her much when it came to the bedroom, but Leah's preaching hadn't much to do with loving-kindness, or mercy and such. No. Leah's righteousness was a battle. She was Jesus's General. If she could command people heavenward then they wouldn't corrupt, wouldn't lie and molder in the grave. With her advanced bombing, her lines of rumbling tanks and machine guns rattling to cover them, they would leap over death at resurrection like soldiers out of foxholes with bayonets fixed. No wonder George turned to drink. He couldn't stand warfare; he couldn't stand the violence of it. He must have seen another kind of Jesus, sweet and gentle, whom Leah had sent AWOL in her preaching. He let the train run over him, and Vida was sure he did it on purpose, or as near to a purpose a man could get while stone drunk in the rain, and tired, tired beyond mention of struggle. George, at least to Vida's way of thinking, didn't die just to get away from Leah. He died to get away from the pain of living.

But Vida would miss him. She wouldn't grieve in the center of her heart but at the edges, where death nibbled away at life the way the creek ate at the banks when the water was high, the way that dishes chipped and cracked and finally broke. He had become a relative in one of the family photographs, one spoken of in the past tense.

* * * * * * * *

As Deborah settled Keith into bed, she asked him, "You realize that it's your Grandpa George who's dead, don't you?"

"Sure I do, Great-granny," Keith answered, expecting to scramble out of his bed and into Franklin's as soon as she left the room.

"That he was your Granny Leah's husband and Ruby's father."

"Course," said Keith. "I ain't dumb."

"I know that," she said. "I just want you to understand. He was your grandfather. I want you to remember."

"I will," he said as she leaned to kiss him goodnight.

"I ain't dumb, neither," Franklin whispered after Deborah had left the room.

"You got epilepsy," said Keith, climbing in beside him. "That's not dumb, just sick. Your underwear is wet. Did you pee in the bed?"

"No, course not. It should of been Jake got cut in half."

"Jake?" said Keith. "Why him?"

"It's him who took her," Franklin answered bitterly.

"Her who?"

"It don't matter," Franklin mumbled, turning his back to the boy.

The unanswered question didn't concern Keith as much as did Franklin's turning away. He more or less clung to Franklin's back, awkwardly trying to hug him, which was difficult in that Franklin was close-armed. "Franklin," he asked desperately, "do you think my Mommy's okay?"

"The old woman's done told you Ruby was down at Leah's."

"Will she come back?"

"Sure," said Franklin. "She ain't dead like George is."

"Where does she go all the time? She ain't never here."

"Work, I reckon."

"I guess so," said Keith, sighing deeply. "But other times, too."

"You don't need them, nohow. I don't."

"But you're growed up," protested Keith.

"You, too. Soon."

"You think so?"

"Sure do," said Franklin, relenting and turning to the boy. "You ticklish?"

"Nah!"

"I bet," said Franklin, who set to proving Keith wrong by scratching the soles of his feet.

In her bedroom on the other side of the house, Deborah listened to the squeals and giggles from Franklin's room. Laughter and death, she thought, laughter and death. But her mind was eased a little by the small joy Keith was bringing to Franklin. She was amazed, though, by how little she felt for the living, or the dead, for that matter, George and James and her three sons departed long ago. Not that she was morbidly concentrating on her own impending death. It sometimes overwhelmed her with its nothingness, a nothingness so intense that the Bible and all its worth paled to insignificance during those moments, those brief periods of illuminating blackness. But they were brief and the Bible was long. There was another emptiness, but it was one of light, and from it came images, mockingbirds and monarch butterflies, the sweet odor of irises and honeysuckle and roses, a breeze on the silver maples along the road, the deep green of the mountains, the clouds and the purest blue. It was the light she concentrated on.

Chapter 5

Keith studied the gnat on the pillow at Deborah's shoulder and shifted from foot to foot. His new white shirt, starched and creased, and buttoned at his throat and wrists, scratched his neck and rubbed his knuckles pink. His frayed belt pinched him, and the waistband of his poplin trousers crimped between the belt loops. From his constricted waist his pants hung formless and baggy, the cuffs lapping onto his stiff brown oxfords which had blistered his heels. He stood in misery beside his great-grandmother on Vida's porch.

But Deborah was comfortable in the place of honor, seated in a heavy lawn chair, a metal rocker painted a vivid green and cushioned with pillows. Shriveled and brown, in a loose, cotton periwinkle dress, she looked both ghastly and sweetly maternal, both a propped-up corpse and a queen. And, as if to match her appearance, her mind drifted from the living to the dead, the dead to the living, with the fitful ease of the wind at an open window, a billowing of life and death with the stirring of soft, voile curtains. Her dead husband James and her brother-in-law Matthew surged gently into the room among the living—among Franklin, Keith and Ruby—and as gently dropped back, floating and white at the window.

The family, of course, thought her mind was bad. Her bridegroom James from 1893 shouldn't be confused with her brother-in-law Matthew from 1918, or either of them with her dead sons, the three of them, or mixing up her dead husband with the recently dead George, her son-in-law. It was an offense to those alive and well, on the Fourth of July, 1946, to think of the dead as equal in importance to those kicking up their heels in the indispensable present. She looked out at her sons and daughters, her in-laws, her grandchildren and great-grandchildren, satisfied with the hurried kiss on the cheek, the moment of chitchat, satisfied with being left in peace, except for the boy at her side, who was a comfort but also an aggravation.

"Keith," she said, "why don't you go take a look at Vida's grapes? They're pretty as the tents of Araby hanging on the wires."

He hesitated for a moment before walking stiffly off the porch, dazed by the sun filtering through the maples, the white table cloths, the clusters of chairs and the people in them, the milling and drifting crowd. He wasn't sure if the noise, which he'd never heard the likes of before, was

109

homey or scary, the clang of horseshoes, the slap of baseball against glove, the tinny music from the Victrola, the children dashing about, squealing and yelling. He wandered among the grapevines, studied the brown shell of a locust on a tree trunk, and was discovered by Sally and Luke, who dragged him into a game of Red Rover with a bunch of cousins he'd never seen before.

Ruby was sitting with a group which included her brother Charles and her aunt Vida. She was passive, scented as the rhododendrons along the creek, shaded among hemlocks, or as yellow orchids in the woods nearby. William was coming to the picnic. Wade had seen him in Riverton and told him about the Fourth. Keith ran up to her, begging to go barefoot. She pulled the boy to her, hugging him in a smothery way. Unaccustomed to such attention and eager to return to his game, he squirmed and asked again, crinkling his nose at her beery, cigarette breath. She agreed. He flipped his shoes off in a second, yanked off his socks, and was gone.

"Don't worry," Charles remarked. "William will be coming with Wade."

Ruby's anticipation was so great she was almost ill. She had already forgiven William everything, and she gave no thought whatsoever to the future, to the fact that he had reenlisted, that he was going off somewhere far, that he might or might not ask her and Keith to go. She didn't want to think or plan or talk. All she wanted was to be with him, to be consumed by the only meaning her life had,

110

which lay in her body like a banked fire, ashes and embers that she wanted to heap passion on as an inexhaustible source of life, to burn in her body with a fire so bright that it blinded her to the day, to Keith, the past, the future, everything but the love which melded her and William into one, timeless and beyond reach, a place where even their bodies vanished, and all was fiery and pure as a dream in which love lost itself in light. She didn't want to wake from the dream, ever.

"What about Ralph?" she asked pensively.

"I warned him off," said Charles. "What do you see in that chucklehead, anyway?"

She wanted to tell her brother that if he hadn't seen what rose between Ralph's legs there wasn't any need explaining. Charles would laugh that low, smutty laugh of his and think she was talking dirty, when in fact she wasn't. "They'll probably fire me at the hotel," she remarked, changing the subject.

"Screw them," he said. "Who needs that nigger work."

He gulped at his beer, stretched his legs and belched, aware of his own good looks and his boredom, bored with Della. It was hell having a wife, especially one who was four months pregnant. He gazed out across the lawn, appreciative of his coal-black shiny hair, his full sensuous face and wiry body. He scanned the grounds several times, searching for a woman he could focus on. But damn! There was nobody but in-laws, though he did think of Ruby, remembering how at Ecco he had danced with her at the Pool Hall, how his dick of its own accord pressed against her thigh, got bone-hard and hurt, being bent down, and how she didn't move away, but danced and shoved against it. He shifted in his chair, raised his right leg and rested it on his knee.

"Ruby, look!" he snorted. "There's Uncle Jake coming down the road. God! Look at Fireball. His damned belly's dragging the ground! We ought to ship the two out west for a Gene Autry movie."

"I don't know who's the biggest horse's ass, that husband of mine or you smart alecks swilling beer," said Vida, laughing as Jake cantered up. "Ride him, Wild Bill!"

Jake trotted into the yard amid derision and urgings-on. Men shouted. Children danced around him, screaming and pointing. The women exclaimed and cautioned. One of the boys threw a firecracker under the horse's legs. When it exploded, the horse shied, whinnying and snorting, and reared. Jake fell off backward as the horse bolted for the pasture, the stirrups flapping at its sides. Women screamed. A crowd of men rushed up. Jake raised himself on his elbows and shook his head. He was helped to his feet. "God damn! I should have been in the cavalry along with Teddy Roosevelt. Where's the little asshole threw that firecracker? I'll break his neck!" Vida brushed his clothes, reminding him that he was a nitwit and it was a wonder his back was still in place.

"Good god!" she said, fussing over him. "You be careful. You'll end up where George is. He's not been dead

two weeks and you falling off a horse trying to kill yourself."

"Shit, Vida," he said. "A horse ain't no train and I
need me a drink of whiskey. Old Fireball and me should of
been with General Grant."

"Christ! Ever man I know's got a cannonball for
brains."

She turned, muttering under her breath, and saw a
bulbous pink Mercury stop at the gate. It was Wade's car,
and William was in the passenger seat. Charles walked out
to them, shouting, "Well, I'll be damned if it ain't the war
hero!" Children rushed over to stare at the bloated auto-
mobile. Ruby and Della came to the gate, followed by Vida.
The crowd paused for a moment to gawk at the car and the
passenger in the Army uniform, the driver in a seersucker
suit and a fedora. Ruby saw immediately that William
hadn't changed. If anything, the Army had disciplined his
shoulders and spine. He fitted perfectly the military cut of
his uniform—the steamy worsted—and stood out among
those at the gate like a statue. He wore his sergeant's
dress uniform in a formal but easy manner. He was clean-
shaven, slightly scented, and somehow pure, innocently
desirable. And blond, with a strong angularity of face, and
with fair unblemished skin and deep-blue eyes, an infre-
quent smile which revealed his straight white teeth. Ruby
went weak in the knees. She trembled, felt helpless.

"Well, god damn!" said Vida in her loudest voice. "If it
ain't the long-lost husband! Where in the hell you been?"

"Leave him alone, Aunt Vida," said Charles. "The man's on furlough."

"It ain't no skin off my nose," she said, slapping William on the arm and hugging him. "Only if his mother-in-law gets ahold of him I ain't responsible."

"Leah said she wasn't coming to the picnic," spoke up Della. "There'd be too much drinking and swearing."

"Come on, William," said Vida, laughing. "You, too, Wade, and get something to eat."

"Not right now," said William awkwardly. "How you been, Charles?"

"Fine," he answered. "Working when I can't get out of it. I got calluses on my knees like a monkey's ass."

"Low coal, huh?" said William.

"Always was, always will be. You remember Crancoal Mine when I first started work and you were straw-boss? Low as that, now."

"Christ," said William. "That was backbreaking."

"Lordamercy, Wade, I ain't seen you since Hereford Creek," said Vida. "Where'd you get that pussy wagon, anyhow?"

She dragged him in her own tactful way to a picnic table, leaving the two young couples—Charles and Della, William and Ruby—to talk among themselves. She piled Wade's plate high; he was the portly type. She opened him a beer.

"Della, you and Ruby are looking fine," said William.

"God," said Della. "I don't know if I'd recognize you on the street, what with that uniform and all."

"Ah," said Charles. "You could recognize Willy Boy anywhere. I bet them Italian women did."

"Shut up, big mouth," said Della. "What do you say we have a beer?"

"You look real fine, William," said Ruby softly.

"The Army's treated me good," he said. "I've decided on it for a career. I've already reenlisted. And it looks like the world's treating you okay."

"Let me holler for Keith," she said, shaken and at a loss.

Della overlooked her sister-in-law's discomfiture. "He's the spitting image of you, William," she said.

"Except he's a runt," Charles remarked.

"You don't expect a Joe Palooka out of a six-year-old," said Della. "He's a good kid, only shier than a deer. I'll go get him."

William looked at the scene in Vida's yard and was depressed by the low ground and heavy shade, the scraggly lawn and ramshackle house, the sagging picnic tables and rusted lawn chairs, the clutter of beer bottles and the slack-mouthed drunks, the squeals and guffaws. Except for a few steady ones like Jake, and he wasn't all that steady, the men had just enough foresight to shirk on the job, get to Riverton for a fifth, and lay hands on the nearest whore. The women cooked the millionth pan of corn bread and pot of beans, raised brats, nagged and bitched. And that was it, no real effort, no future, nothing to show for the labor. He felt as if he had walked into a reunion of derelicts. On Hereford Creek, with the Dingesses nearby— Leah and George—Ruby had paced in front of the door like a bitch in heat, almost whining for a hand at the knob, anything to get herself away, out of the house, anything to get her among her brother, her numberless cousins and kin, not for another man but for swarming with her relations like gnats over creek water. But he was determined to try again, to start over, and the only way to do it was to take her and Keith away, to Fort Ord or wherever else the Army might station him. Della tugged and pushed Keith forward. The boy was in a state of mortification, dragging his feet and twisting his head about.

"Look at that," said Charles. "You'd think we was going to bust his ass."

"Here, Keith," said Ruby, gesturing to him. "Come say hello to your Daddy."

"Cat's got his tongue," said Charles.

Keith looked up at his father, the strange man towering in front of him, at his visored hat, like a dark halo against the sky, at his shirt and tie, at his coat with the stiff epaulets and lapels, the shiny buttons and the belt of his coat. And though he wasn't capable of imagining much—he'd never been out of the hollow to speak of—what he lacked in detail he made up for in awe of the man from the world beyond, for the wonder of far-off distances. He saw his father in the glow of horizons, so light-filled that he

116

appeared transparent, and within his outline was the unknown sublimity of the future. Keith knew that he was linked to this man, and that his destiny would be different from the others in the yard. He knew it instantly, unconsciously, and felt more comfortable with himself.

"You all set down," said Della, "and I'll get some beers. Keith, you want a pop?"

"A orange," he whispered.

"I'll bring it," she said.

"Hello, Keith," said William.

"Say hello, honey," said Ruby. "And you can call him Daddy."

"Hi," Keith managed.

"So, you going to school in the fall?"

Keith nodded his head.

"Well, since you are," said William, taking out his wallet and handing Keith a ten dollar bill, "you'll need some money for notebooks and pencils."

Charles smiled, knowing how loose a soldier on furlough was with money. William would spend a couple hundred before he left, and Charles could loaf for a week with an old buddy from the Army. No one at the mines would begrudge him a day or two, certainly not his uncle Jake.

William glanced at Keith and smiled, reassured. He had none of that black-haired, brown-eyed look, none of that roundness of face, though he found such features appealing in Ruby. They somehow suited a woman, if her skin were not too brown, and Ruby was hardly ever in the sun. But not in a man, that softness which sometimes reminded him of punk wood, like Charles. Della brought the drinks and all but Keith sat down. He was too astonished. He'd never had more than a dime in his hand. To be holding a ten dollar bill was breathtaking.

"What's them hawks on your buttons for?" he asked, taking heart.

"Those are eagles. They stand for our country."

"And everybody's happy when it takes a shit," said Charles.

"What?"

"Nothing, Keith," said Della, who turned to her husband. "Shut up, goofy."

"Did you get a purple heart for being brave?"

"I don't know about that, but I did get wounded."

"Where at?"

"In the chest and ribs. Shrapnel."

"What's that?" Keith asked, wanting to see the wounds, but not if his father had to muss his uniform.

"It's a bomb that blows up and scatters pieces of metal."

"Similar to a shotgun blowing up in your face, Keith," said Charles.

"It sure as hell is," said William bitterly, thinking of the grotesque scars across his chest, deforming the symmetry of his pectorals. A nipple was missing.

"Oh," said Keith with a shudder. "But your purple heart sure is purple. Who's picture is in the heart?"

"I don't know. I never asked."

"What's them little guns for?"

"I was in the infantry. I still am, but I work with field equipment, now. Radio transmitters, things like that."

"Wade said you was being transferred to California," Charles remarked.

"To Fort Ord," said William. "I have to be there on the fifteenth."

"Lord," said Della. "How come you ain't been around before now?"

"You know how family is," said William lamely.

"Is that out at the ocean?" Keith asked.

"What?" said William. "Oh, you mean California. Yes, the Pacific Ocean."

"Jesus Christ," Charles complained. "Is that all the kid can do, ask questions?"

"You leave him be," said Della, reaching out to hug him around the waist. She was thinking of her own baby on the way.

"I guess you heard that Daddy got killed," said Charles.

"Yes," said William. "Wade told me. I always liked George."

"How a man could be stupid enough as to set down on the railroad tracks and get run over is beyond me," said

Charles. "Only thing I can figure is he was drunk and passed out."

"Mrs. Dingess ain't taking it too good," remarked Della, who was baffled by the family she'd married into, both families, actually, since it included Charles's aunt Vida, whose picnic they were at. Charles Dingess talked about his father George as if he were just some coal miner who happened to have gotten killed, not somebody close, and George's daughter Ruby hadn't made much effort one way or another about grieving. But not George's wife, not Leah Dingess. If she was crabby before, she was now a flogging hen slinging Bibles like burning skillets.

"Knocked the wind out of her is all," said Charles. "That mother of mine will be back to preaching soon enough." He was proud, in a perverse way, that his mother was a woman preacher and known over most of three counties.

"Keith, honey, you want to go back and play?" said Ruby. "This is all just grownup talk. And thank your Daddy for the money."

"Thank you."

"You want to hug your Daddy?"

"He's too big for that," said William quickly, "but maybe he'd like to shake hands."

William leaned in the chair and Keith reached forward, his hand disappearing in his father's. He let his hand drop to his side when William relaxed his grip. He knew well enough that he was being dismissed, and confused by disappointment and relief, a tremor of anxiety crossed his face. The man sitting before him could never be his Daddy. He could never come down and live among his mother's people. They wouldn't allow an eagle—like the eagles on his chest—among themselves, but would harry and cry until it soared beyond a ridge and disappeared. Keith felt the grief already, the streams of gray clouds at the peaks. He wanted to be there in the streaming clouds. And he realized suddenly that his mother wouldn't go with his father out to California. She might go somewhere with the other man, with Ralph, or somebody close to home, but not with him. He watched his father tilt his head back and drink beer, watched as his adam's apple moved up and down. He saw the brown eagle, saw its broad wings on the updraft, heard its dangerous, piercing cry, *eeee.*

"You go play, now, honey," said Ruby. "Put your money in your pocket. You don't want to lose it."

Keith picked up his socks and shoes and walked dejectedly to the porch. He laid them aside, watching as Charles and Della left his parents to themselves. He saw his father lean toward his mother, the two of them talking privately. He was afraid they would disappear, that he would see them mingling in the crowd, that he would turn away for a piece of watermelon, or to fan the dry ice under the ice cream to watch the smoke, and they would be gone, inexplicably and maybe forever. He sat on the porch beside his great-grandmother. He knew they would leave, but he had to know when and in what direction. He knew

121

soon enough. They climbed into the Mercury with the man in the striped suit and left the hollow. Della came to Keith. "They just went for a drive," she said, though she knew that Wade was taking his parents to the hotel. "They'll be back." She tousled his hair and returned to Charles, feeling sorry for Keith and knowing that she would beat the daylights out of any tramp her man might take to a place like that. She went to the Pool Hall to keep track of his wandering hands, and besides, she knew the church drove a wedge between too many couples. She wasn't going to let that happen to her and Charles, church or no church, and maybe she could keep him from drinking so much.

Keith felt Deborah's fingertips on his shoulder, alongside his neck, and presently on his cheek, dry and bony, caressing his temple and cheek. He sighed and relaxed, knowing where she was without having to look and keep watch over.

Deborah, with her eyes closed, was not thinking particularly of Keith, or of Matthew or her first son, who had slipped away from home in 1917, going off with General Pershing's troops to France and getting himself killed, or her two sons killed in the mines over in Raleigh County in 1925, Or of Franklin, whom she'd never touched in the way she was touching Keith. She sighed, trying not to worry about the boy. She could feel the soft fleshiness of his cheek, the warm downy life against her fingertips. It felt very far away, as though a child were tugging at her sleeve. Which child? she puzzled. Which child plucked at her apron while she was peeling potatoes, sprinkling clothes for ironing, and what could it want but to fuss and whine? She withdrew her hand and pulled her arms close to her chest.

"Keith, darling," she said, "maybe you ought to go play. We wouldn't want the other children to think I was making over you."

"Well, I guess," he said.

He walked off the porch. Sally and Luke involved him in a game of Hide-and-Seek. Luke leaned against a tree and counted, his forearm over his face. Keith ran to the back of the house and flattened himself behind the outcrop of sandstone at the creek.

Vida had watched Ruby and William leave, and her feelings were mixed. At least, she thought as she sliced watermelon, her niece was going off with a man who was her own husband, for once, and there was no denying that he was handsome, not to her tastes, precisely, since he seemed more like a man going to a parade field than one coming to court a woman, and he took his time about it, too, since the word was he had been at Coalton for nearly a week, and out of a thirty-day leave, that didn't bespeak much of an interest in Ruby, not to mention Keith. And Vida knew Ruby. She knew that Ruby would never say a word about him leaving her destitute, him joining the Army as a single man and sending no allotment for her and Keith. It was Vida's bet that Mary Brousek, or Ivan himself, lit into William and shamed him into coming to see

Ruby. Vida didn't know the Brouseks well, but she knew they had a streak of decency, however much old man Ivan might tear and cuss, especially when he was drinking. Whatever brought William up the hollow, he would have to face Leah's wrath. Vida didn't see how he could avoid it, unless Ruby got to her first and warned her not to ruin a new chance at married life. As for Vida, if she were in Ruby's shoes, she would have kicked William's ass the minute he walked through the gate. But she wasn't Ruby, and since there was no altering character, she let her niece be and went on about her own business. But no man would treat her that way. Jake had slapped her once. Afterwards, when he was sitting on the edge of the back porch, she sneaked up behind and cold-cocked him with an iron skillet. When he came to, she told him that, if he ever hit her again, she would catch him off-guard, as she did with the skillet, only the next time he wouldn't be able to find his balls. She would have blown them into the creek with the shotgun. Jake never slapped her again.

Diagonally across the creek, flat on his stomach behind a rhododendron, was Franklin, whose view of the house was complete but for the lower front and the far side. The notion of spying was almost a compensation for the envy which gnawed at him worse than his empty stomach. He knew he wasn't stupid. He observed the goings-on in the yard, and it pleased him to think of surprising Keith with what he knew. He was jealous of the children who included Keith in their game, and it disturbed

124

him to see the boy lying so close by. He watched for a moment, then wriggled along the bank until he was directly across from the jutting sandstone.

"Keith!" he called out in a whisper, and the boy looked up bewilderedly. "Over here! Look!"

"Franklin! What are you doing—"

"Shh! Come over here. I seen everything."

Keith pulled his baggy pant legs up past his knees, waded the creek, and clambered into the thicket, happy to see his friend. He thought of himself as a Kraut spying on the house, or a Jap.

"Vida better not catch you," he whispered.

"She won't," said Franklin. "Nobody can when I don't want them to."

"Did you see my Daddy? He's in the Army."

"Sure did. Him and Ruby went off."

"I know," breathed Keith, unsure, now, if he were jealous or relieved of a burden.

"I'm hungry," said Franklin. "Can you get me a plate?"

"I guess so," Keith answered uncertainly. "I guess I can sneak it around. What do you want?"

"Some of everything," answered Franklin.

Franklin scooted further into the bushes and Keith started across the creek. Luke found him as he was midstream and shouted that he weren't playing fair; he weren't supposed to hide outside the yard. He cheated and he couldn't play any more, and that reduced Keith's difficulties by one. And nobody paid any attention to him at the picnic

125

table; they had eaten and the dishes were covered. As Keith filled a plate he realized that he would have to make two trips, which turned out fairly simple but for the fuss of rolling his britches legs up and down twice. His last trip included Kool-Aid, chocolate pie and watermelon. His nerves settled as he crouched in the bushes, and with the satisfaction of a grown-up caring for a needy, appreciative child, he watched Franklin eat.

"You coming home this evening?" asked Franklin, wiping his mouth on his sleeve.

"Yes. I'm coming home with Great-granny. You know my Daddy gave me a whole ten dollars?"

"He did?"

"Yes," said Keith. "Here, look."

He pulled the bill out of his pocket and Franklin stared.

"I never saw one, before," he said.

"It's for school," said Keith, tucking it carefully away.

"School? Can you go from up at the house?"

"Sure," said Keith. "It ain't a far walk to Ecco."

"I better get up the hollow," said Franklin.

"Well. We'll be home after while."

Franklin disappeared in the rhododendrons and Keith, after he crossed the stream with the cup and dishes, sat for awhile on the bedrock. He didn't need those silly kids, Luke and Sally or any of the others. The noise from the front of the house, the subdued pandemonium, seemed to Keith to come from another world, another place, and had

126

very little to do with him. The anxiety concerning his mother still edged at him with its unhappiness, yet he sensed it as temporary, as if he understood that she would always return. But in a place in his mind where knowing is unknown, he realized that his father was lost to him forever, that he wasn't actually a person to want for the presence of, but a need for which he would never experience fulfillment, for which he would never know happiness, comfort, disappointment or pain. His father was alive, though, and the faint hope for love was a slow, aching torment, a need which he wouldn't cry about, since the unknowing in his mind knew the futility of weeping.

Franklin crossed the creek well above Vida's house, stepped into the road and ran home. It was seldom that he was by himself in the house. The quiet unsettled him and quickened his pulse. He hurried into Deborah's room where Ruby kept her clothes. He knelt by the bed and picked up her shoes, the black pumps and the white sandals. He stroked them, kissed the leather and smelled the insides. Replacing the shoes, he stepped over to the bureau and opened a drawer, touching her underwear, the silky brassieres and panties. He opened the chifforobe and fondled her dresses, undoing the zippers and taking them off the hangers, putting them to his face, his lips. He returned them and went to the dresser, picking up her talcum powder, her rouge, lipstick, her perfume, the heart-shaped, deep-purple bottle.

He removed the stopper very carefully, placed his left palm over the opening, and quickly tilted the bottle. He re-stoppered it and placed it back on the dresser. He ran with his fist clinched, hoarding the guilty pleasure of sweet musk, and in the far recesses of the barn, which had been transformed by the afternoon sun to a soft, dusky gold, he put his left hand to his face, his right hand reaching to the brass buttons of his fly, and was in an ecstasy of silent and solitary love.

Chapter 6

Wade guided his Mercury like a huge pink slug down the hollow. He had his hand on the seat between himself and Ruby, who was so pretty that everything about a gorgeous woman blended into her. He got a tingling between his legs thinking about it, William or no William. Keith, on bent knees in the back, was hanging over the front seat between Wade and Ruby. Wade liked the boy, but wished he'd disappear.

Ecco, when they finally got there, was so different a place that Keith figured they must have traveled a hundred miles. He also decided, instantly, that it was the ugliest, blackest place on earth. Up ahead, against a steep ridge, squatted the coal tipple, a huge tinny box, its sidings fanning out like the legs of a giant crab. The foremen's houses sat atop a tree-lined embankment, stolid, two-story and white. Across from them the Island Creek Store reared up; and beyond it, in a bottom, stretched six rows of company houses, gray and low to the ground. Slate was everywhere. It sprawled from the dump sites on the mountain; it was heaped behind the company houses, huge gob piles which ignited and burned, demonic as the hell his Grandmother Leah preached about, black mounds from which smoke coiled in gray ropes. A white pall hung over the coal camp, and the odor was sulfurous. Beyond the rows of houses was the river, silted by the washers on the tipple which tainted the water black.

Wade parked alongside a row of two-story, brick buildings which faced the highway and the C&O tracks. Two were vacant; the others contained a hardware store, a clothing store, a furniture store, a beauty parlor and the Ecco Pool Hall.

Peeking in the windows, Keith was agog at the axes, shovels and wheelbarrows, the sparkling pots and pans, the dishes, the shelf after shelf of mysterious cans and cartons, the living room suites and beds and bureaus, the tables, chairs, lamps and light fixtures. Wade and Ruby could hardly drag him down the street. He was amazed by the cars rushing past, most of them black, sleek and glittering. The pedestrians looked to him more dressed-up than they would be for church; they smelled of perfume and lotion. Coal dust covered the parked cars and spiraled from the edge of the highway as automobiles sped past. The dust left a stinky taste in his mouth. He was suddenly anxious. His mother's lips were too red, her hair in funny bangs on her forehead and hanging in loopy curls on her dress collar, her face too white, her smell too sweet. It almost choked him. "That's *Evening In Paris*, honey," she had said. Her dress was shiny green, tight-belted, and made a slithery noise when she walked. And the strange man, Wade, kept hogging the sidewalk.

"Come on, boy," said Wade. "When we get inside, I'll show you a trick."

He shuffled alongside them, but at the tavern he was amazed by the neon sign. He pulled loose from his mother's hand, and wiping the sweat on his pants, he ran to the window. *Ecco* was spelled in a soft glowing blue, and the words *Pool Hall* in flushed red. The sign was one long tube of glass, about the size of his finger, curved to spell out the letters. His mother yanked him inside. He pinched his nose in the damp, sourish air and blinked, gaping at the smoky, brownish-gray room, the bar in the center, a row of booths on one side, a row of tables on the other. Pictures with soft lights and mirrors hung above the bar, pictures of beer bottles, teams of horses, smiling women, cigarette packs, men in automobiles. Ruby pulled him to the table where his father sat with Vida and Jake, Charles and Della. He was shocked to see his father out of uniform and in an ordinary white shirt and slacks. He was also disappointed to see him slouched, his blond hair disheveled, the blueness of his eyes blurred over, and his smile crooked. Charles was slouchy, too; Keith didn't like him much, but he liked Della. She was pretty, not

131

dressed-up the way his mother was, and she smiled at him. William moved his chair around and Ruby sat at his side. Wade squeezed a chair in beside Charles and Della, his left haunch not quite on the seat, and he felt for a moment the old despair of never quite fitting in, of never truly belonging, never having a real friend or a woman, no matter how much he tried. He tugged uncomfortably at the lapels of his seersucker coat, loosened his tie and unbuttoned his collar.

"Sorry we're late," said Ruby, "but Granny Deborah ain't feeling too good, and Mommy was fussing."

"She's always fussing," said Charles. "That mother of ours is a regular demon since Dad got killed. The way I figured it, she wouldn't give a damn."

"We was all wrong there," said Della.

"Wade," said William, handing him a twenty dollar bill, "get us some more beer." William didn't like having to think about Leah. She was mean-tempered and ugly as a snapping turtle.

"Maybe some pork rinds," said Ruby, "and some pickled pigs' feet."

"And some pickled eggs," said Della.

Wade struggled out of his chair and Keith followed him to the bar, asking to be shown the trick. Wade lifted him onto a bar stool and set him spinning. When the stool slowed, Keith grasped the counter and twirled himself in the opposite direction. The bartender put a Coca-Cola and potato chips in front of him, and Wade carried the beer and snacks to the table.

"A grieving woman ought to sit around and mope, not hiss like a cat up a tree," Charles grumbled. "She ain't taking it like a Christian."

"Maybe that's her problem," Della remarked.

"Problem, how's that?" asked Charles.

"Look at that boy spin," said Wade. "Just like a top." Wade didn't care much for Mrs. Dingess, either. The men at the mine office called her the circuit rider from hell. That was on everybody's tongue, a crazy woman to joke about, but whenever her name was mentioned so was Ruby's, and the talk got dirty. Wade hadn't been at Ecco long, but he knew that Ruby wasn't all that bad. It was in comparison to her preacher mother that she seemed that way.

"Well," said Della, "she's my mother-in-law, so it ain't for me to say much, but it might be she's feeling guilty."

"Her off preaching you mean?" asked Ruby.

"Yeah," said Della, "and her getting off a train the very evening Mr. Dingess got run over by one."

"Shit," said Charles. "That was just chance."

"Course it was," said William, chuckling. "She didn't run over him."

"Oh, come on, you two," said Della. "I mean guilty because she was running from George to God, and God told her it wasn't right by taking George away."

"Oh, crap, Della," Charles griped. "You sound like a preacher woman yourself. How do you know all that?"

"I got a brain," she said. "And I go to church now and then."

"Fuck," said Charles. "God didn't have nothing to do with it. Booze did, and a train and a railroad track."

"I'm not saying that God took George away. I'm saying that Leah might believe it. And there's more, too. The woman's going through the—"

"I got a joke to tell you all," said Wade, butting in. "There was a woman who bet her boyfriend she could piss higher up on the wall than him. He bet with her, so she whipped off her drawers, laid down on the floor and let a stream fly three feet high. 'Shit,' said the boyfriend, 'I can beat that by a mile!' He whipped out his dork, but just as he started to piss she hollered, 'No hands!'"

Everybody had heard the joke before, but they guffawed anyway, glad to be off the subject of Leah. Keith, his hands and mouth greasy from the potato chips, swiveled to look at the grownups laughing at the table. He turned back to his Coca-Cola and belched, an oily, fizzy sensation in his nostrils. Wade, from where he was sitting, saw Ruby move her hand so that it rested between William's legs. He also saw that Vida was drinking an RC Cola. He thought that odd until he noticed that Jake was nearly passed out in his chair. Jake had taken a couple of shots of William's whiskey, on top of all the beer he had drunk.

"Wade!" Keith called. "Let's me and you do something."

"You come over here," said Wade. "I'll tell you what's great you can do."

Keith jumped off the bar stool and ran over. Wade whispered in his ear.

"Nah," said Keith. "Mommy won't let me do that."

"Do what, honey?" asked Ruby.

"Nothing," said Wade. He put his arm around Keith, pulled him close and whispered to him, and then said, "Now, you go on. Start over there where they can't see you."

Keith walked sheepishly to the other side of the bar and approached a group of strangers. He mumbled, "I'm really thirsty."

A man in a white shirt turned to him. His hair was greasy and the pores in his face were black. "What's that, kid?" he asked.

"I'm thirsty," Keith mumbled, gulping. "Could you give me a nickel for a pop?"

"Get your little ass out of here," the man said. "You don't belong in no beer joint."

Keith was mortified. He started to turn away.

"Oh, give him a nickel, tight-ass," said the woman sitting beside the man. "And he needs more than a nickel." She turned to the next booth and shouted, "Hey, Clarissa! Get them tightwads over there to give this boy a nickel!"

Keith was beginning to appreciate the generosity of drunks when, by the fourth booth, he had collected thirty-five cents. But his begging ended with a commotion on the other side of the room. He rounded the end of the bar just in time to see his Granny Dingess raise her arms. He shrank back, attempting to hide behind a stool.

"The Lord's wrath will descend on you!" she screamed.

"Oh, wrath's ass, Mommy," said Charles. "How'd you get down here, anyway?"

"The Lord seen to it!" she shouted.

"It was more like them fast feet of yours, I reckon," he said.

"You heathens are wallowing in a pit of hell, a den of debauchery, a sink-hole of sin! My very own children!"

"Amen, Sister!" yelled William, who was thoroughly drunk.

"Hush up, you hunky! What I got to say to you ain't fit to be spoken! It's you who's dragged my daughter down!"

"Mommy!" exclaimed Ruby. "I'm married to the man."

"Mrs. Dingess," said Della, starting to rise. "Maybe me and you ought to go to the ladies' room."

"You just stay put," said Leah, reaching across Charles to push her down. "I'm here to show you what sin is. Sin is liquor!"

"Amen!" shouted William.

Ruby giggled. Everyone in the tavern turned to look at the shouting woman. Some of the customers grumbled and booed, but several of them, in a spirit akin to William's, urged her on. "You tell it, Sister! You can tell it!"

"Sin is lust!" Leah screamed. "It's Delilah! Sheba!"

"Yes!"

"David and the Elders!"

"Yeah!"

"Potiphar's wife! Lot's wife!"

"Amen!"

"Maybe you can't see the sin in yourselves!" Leah shouted. "Maybe you need somebody to show it to you!"

She grabbed Ruby's Strohs and guzzled. There was an astonished silence for a moment, then Ruby squealed, "Mommy!"

"I'll be shit!" Charles shouted. "Look at her chugalugging that beer!"

Leah slammed the empty bottle down on the table. Jake woke from his stupor, saw Leah, rolled his eyes and closed them again. "Where's the bottle?" she shouted. William reached to the floor and handed her the fifth. She drank and began to rave, "My children have worried me gray-headed and flayed my nerves like a mule's hide. They've sassed and disobeyed and swarped around till I'm thin as a rail and half sick night and day. They're just like their Daddy and him dead, now, and gone to hell. And he went of his own accord, not mine. But I'm going to show you sin." And she gulped at the whiskey once more.

"Have at it, preacher woman!" someone shouted from across the bar. "Hallelujah them right to hell!"

"I prayed till my knees was sore. I got laryngitis from praying, thinking it was a lack in me, and it was, it was! It was the drying up of the soul, the drying up of blood! Christ's blood! Last night He called to me. He cried out crucified that the entire world—not just my children!—but the whole world was on that wide road to hell. And I'm preaching on it. I stand here as a warning. This is my willed duty, mine! To show you sin and lust!"

Keith, behind the bar stool, had a vision of his grandmother in the middle of the street outside the tavern, swinging a huge cross like a battle-ax as pedestrians tried to pass.

"Do you know what the Red Sea is?" she thundered.

"Only been to the Ohio, myself!" someone shouted.

"Come on, Mrs. Dingess," said Della, reaching out to grab her. "That's enough."

"No, it ain't enough!" Leah bellowed hoarsely, snatching Wade's Schlitz and gulping it down. "It's pain, that's what it is, and you can't know pain till you've been outcast. Well I'm crossing over. I'm going to meet Moloch, and Magog, too, and Jezebel. My only pain's been grief. I ain't never been in the depths. And you ain't been in the pit, neither, none of you! You're digging little mud holes in the ground. Till now, all my worries been sickly, and all my Jesus Lights been in the broad of day. But it's only in the blackest night His shining face—oh, Glory, Glory!—only in the blackest pit does His Light shine meaningful."

"Shit, woman!" shouted the man with the greasy hair. "You come with me to Number 3 Mine and I'll show you what a hellpit is!"

"Charles, let me out of here," said Della. "We got to get her back up the hollow."

"Now I'm going to show you lust!" Leah shrieked.

"It's about fucking time!" shouted a drunk two tables away.

"We got to stop her," said Ruby in a hushed voice.

"No," said William, his hand gripping her shoulder. "Stay out of it."

"Just let her be," said Vida. "She's having her day."

"Her day?" said Ruby.

Vida didn't answer. Leah staggered to the bar, her bony frame wobbling like a skeleton in a cotton print dress. She put her hands on the counter and lifted a knee onto a bar stool, but as she put her weight on it, the stool spun around and she ended in the middle of the floor, turning clockwise.

"Move, Wade!" shouted Della.

Before Wade could stir the bulk of his heavy body, Leah made a running leap and skidded on her belly onto the bar, collecting bottles and ashtrays in her outstretched arms as she slid down the length of it. Keith ducked and ran to his mother.

"My god, the woman can fly!" someone cheered from the other side of the bar.

Leah stood up, banging her head against a Miller's beer sign hanging from the ceiling. The pale yellow light glowed cadaverously on her face. She patted her hair seductively and thrust out a hip. "I'm going to show you lust," she croaked. The tendons pulled tautly at her throat as she tilted her head in a haughty pose. Jerkily, she began a bump-and-grind, slowly pulling up her dress. She revealed her skinny calves and knobby knees before Wade made a grab at her. She skipped away, moving along the counter in a can-can to avoid him. The bartender, on his side of the counter, moved with Wade, on the customers' side, to form a kind of chorus line, shuffling with her as she sashayed up and down the bar.

"My god!" said Della, trying to loosen Charles's grip on her elbow. "I knew your all's mother was peculiar, but this beats everything!"

"What's she doing!?" Keith wailed.

"They'll get her down, honey, don't worry," said Ruby, "and then we can take her home."

"You better take her to the nut house," said William.

Della stomped Charles's ankle. "Let me out!"

"Hunh," he groaned. "Jesus, woman, take it easy!"

"Mrs. Dingess, get down from there!" Della yelled, extricating herself from the chair. "You're making a horse's ass of yourself."

Leah had hiked her dress up to her thighs and was doing high-kicks as she skipped along the bar. On one of her turns she skidded in a puddle of beer and fell off

140

backward into Wade's arms. Sighs of relief went up in the room, groans of disappointment, catcalls, whistles, applause.

"Charles!" the bartender shouted. "You get your mother home, now, and don't come back till you do!"

Keith ran up to look. His Granny Leah was limp in Wade's arms. Her eyes were rolling in her head. Saliva dribbled from her lower lip. She was mumbling incoherently and waving her arms. Della pulled at her dress. Ruby and Vida helped Wade stand her upright.

"Let's take her out the back way," said Ruby. "Wade, you bring your car around."

They left Jake sitting at the table, stone drunk as ever. Charles and William led Leah up the alley. The women and Keith followed behind. With her arms around the men's shoulders, Leah got the hiccups, and with each jerk of her scarecrow frame she shouted *Praise God, Hallelujah!* She staggered in a wobbly, jerky manner. Vida started to giggle, then Ruby and Della.

"Hush up, you all!" Charles harrumphed. "Ain't you got no respect for my mother?"

"I respect her dancing," said Vida. "It's the Charleston them knees of hers is doing. Flapping in the wind. My sister's dancing could heal the sick. It could raise the dead."

"Shit!" Charles groaned, staggering under the weight. He couldn't help laughing.

Vida began to prance around them, twisting her hips, skipping, clapping her hands. Ruby and Della laughed and joined in. Keith leaped and ran in circles around them, also, gibbering like a monkey.

"You crazy fools," said William. "They're going to cart us all off to the bug house."

Vida tickled William under the arms, and helpless to prevent her, his chuckling rose to an uncontrollable laugh. Della goosed him. He whooped and skipped, nearly losing his grip on Leah's waist. As they crossed the weedy rise to Wade's car, Charles tripped on a clump of grass and fell, dragging his mother and William down in his fall. Ruby yelled and leaped onto the pile. Vida grabbed Keith and leaped also. Della followed. There was squalling and braying and laughter.

"God dammit, will you all get off of me!" Charles's muffled shout came from the bottom of the pile.

"Is Mommy still breathing?" asked Ruby, untangling herself and sitting up.

"Sure she is," said Vida. "Ain't nothing wrong with her but what a little dancing on a bar didn't cure."

She grabbed Leah by the arms and pulled her to a sitting position. They untangled themselves and rose, Charles and William lifting Leah between themselves again. She had a glazed, uncomprehending look in her eyes. They brushed the straw off her dress and trundled on toward Wade's pink Mercury.

"I think you can take her home from here," Ruby said to Wade.

"You all ain't coming?" he asked, feeling as if Ruby had hit him in the stomach.

"There ain't no need to," she answered. "You don't mind, do you?"

"I reckon not," said Wade, "but ain't you worried about her?"

"Nothing to worry about," said Charles. "She'll sleep it off."

"Keith, honey," said Ruby, bending to kiss the boy on the cheek, "you go on with Wade. He'll take you to your Great-granny's. Don't tell her what happened to your Granny Leah, okay? Deborah ain't been feeling too good, you know, and she'd just worry."

"I wouldn't tell her," said Keith. "It was nasty."

They helped Leah into the back seat, where she immediately stretched out and began to snore. As Wade pulled away, Keith watched the others amble back to the Pool Hall. He sat on his knees, riding backward, peering over the seat at his grandmother.

"You get yourself any money?" asked Wade.

"Seven nickels," Keith answered, "but my Daddy gave me a ten-dollar bill on the Fourth of July."

"He did?"

"Yes. Do you think she'll die?"

"Her? No, but with her hangover she'll probably wish she had. Maybe she won't remember nothing. Did your Daddy tell you about the war? He was in Italy."

"He did some, and he showed me his Purple Heart."

"That's good. You all going to California?"

"Don't know."

"Your Mommy didn't say?"

"Nope."

"Me and you in the same boat, you know that?"

"How come?"

"Ah, nothing."

"I like his uniform," said Keith.

"Yeah, it's fine."

Wade turned off the highway and crossed the tracks. As he started up the hollow, Keith shifted and faced forward, breathing more easily as the mountains closed in on each side of the road. He caught glimpses of the creek between the trees. But he slumped down as they passed his Great-uncle Jake's place. He didn't like Danny or Beulah. Looking up, he saw the forced smile on Wade's face, his arm as he waved to someone in the yard. After the car passed the house, he stared through the windshield at the overhanging branches and the leaves. Fragments of the sun blurred glitteringly and shimmered among the green, which took his mind momentarily off his mother and father.

Wade watched as the boy trudged up the path to his great-grandmother's. He turned the car and drove back down the hollow, glancing frequently over his shoulder at the woman sprawled in the back seat. He knew the Dingesses used him as a taxi, and so did William. Ruby used him. He saw himself giving jelly beans to a group of children who snatched the bag out of his hand. He was their taxi, sure enough, and this time he was carrying a bucket of bones. There was a bitter taste in his mouth, although, as he glanced over his shoulder, looking at the woman on her back, her head propped on the arm rest, her knees bent and her legs spread, her dress up around her thighs, his penis swelled tightly in his trousers. "God," he muttered, "I'd rather go to the barn." As he passed Jake's place again, he smiled his forced smile and waved. It was Vida's Beulah and Danny he was waving at, and Leah's Josephine, a girl so sexed-up it was a wonder she didn't explode. He would dump Leah off at her house and return to the Pool Hall, if she didn't puke all over him, first.

Franklin was sitting slump-shouldered at the bottom of the steps, as dejected as the boy walking up to him, since both felt left behind, Franklin by Keith and Keith by his parents. Keith sat down beside his friend and sighed. They were forlorn.

"You was gone about all day," complained Franklin.

"It wasn't no fun," Keith replied. "I almost got sick, and Granny Leah, she got drunk."

"I got potatoes yet to hoe," said Franklin, indifferent to Leah. "The sun's mostly off. You want to help?"

"I chop the plants down, you said."

"You willing to squash potato bugs?"

"Only with the glove."

"Okay," said Franklin. "I'll get it."

They smiled and got up to work. Keith made it down one row and halfway up another, but he got so tired he just had to rest. He carried Franklin's water jar to an old apple tree by the fence, had himself a drink, counted his nickels, and in a minute or two was asleep. Franklin smiled and kept hoeing. It was the kind of work he liked, the rhythmical striking of the hoe that calmed the beating of his heart and settled his mind, the peaceableness as he let his hoe blade strike with just enough force to pierce the surface and slice through the roots of the weeds. Then he piled the dirt around the potato stems, tugging loose soil up under the plants, which were getting bushy.

Franklin's mind often skittered with half-thoughts, startling and unformed ideas, frightening concepts which he glimpsed as they disappeared in the darkness he couldn't see to the source of, a nothingness where most people dwelt, and from which they talked and left him puzzled and in dread, as if what they spoke he needed to comprehend but couldn't, it being so dark where they were, a place so filled with screams not screamed, whispers not whispered, wants not wanted that it seemed they might destroy themselves any minute, because what they said wasn't what their eyes said, or their faces, or their shoulders and hands. What did God mean, or Jesus, or mother, or father, or love? He had heard the words often enough, but they vibrated with need, pain, and anger. He turned away and hoed the garden, and there he was at peace.

* * * * * * * *

Vida and the others returned to the Pool Hall, sobered a little after the outrageous fit Leah threw and, well, after their own fit in the alley, and it was led by Vida, too, the sober one in the group, who should have been acting shocked and distressed, instead of whooping it up like an escapee from an asylum led by a backsliding preacher, who happened to be out of her mind, herself, the skinniest hoochie-koochie dancer this side of Egypt. The bartender had cleaned up the mess; he had also moved Jake to a booth in the back facing the wall, where he was curled up like an overgrown infant on the seat. Vida shrugged and figured what the hell; they could drag him home later. She could drink a beer or two, maybe even a shot of whiskey out of the fifth William had hidden in a poke, if there was any left after Leah had at it. She hated soda pop.

"Della," she said as they settled at the table, "you oughtn't have throwed yourself on that pile of drunks back there. You're pregnant."

The young woman laughed. "I couldn't resist, Vida," she said. "Besides, I was on the top."

William went to the bar and ordered beer, and then to the men's room. Charles asked Ruby to dance. Vida

147

sighed deeply and patted Della on the hand. "Leah is going through the change," she said, "but I don't think she feels much guilt about George getting killed. That was you talking. You would feel guilty, but not my sister. She would think it was his fit punishment. You know, the wages of sin."

Della understood that the sisters fought, so she was a bit distrustful of what Vida was saying. "Why is she acting so crazy, then?" she asked. "Maybe backsliding is her punishment on herself."

"I doubt it," said Vida. "My sister likes to show off. People will think her drinking is because of grief, wild grief, her desperation and such, being hopeless, if you know what I mean, or you thinking it's because of guilt, and it may be, it may be both, but for my part I think it's mostly to show off. Leah always did like a crowd, in church or in a beer joint."

The juke box ended with Red Foley, and after a grinding, clicking noise, took up with Roy Acuff. William returned from the men's room and danced with Ruby. Charles danced with Della. Vida complained to herself because Jake—dammit—was passed out and she didn't have a partner. She sighed and drank her beer, watching Ruby dance. Ruby was in a world like seventh heaven, Vida could tell that. The way she wrapped her body around William would make the woman who popped out of a cake blush. She was a snake charmer making the snake rise, a snake with a man attached, and him probably not important but for the pleasure the snake could give, not what the man was but what he had, and Vida was sure that William had a hard-on, the way he was pressing up between Ruby's legs. The horny bastard. He didn't pay any attention to his son, and Keith was the only one he had.

She looked away and stared at the Camel sign above the bar. She felt she was right about what she had said to Della. Leah was a show-off. She used to flounce around Daddy James just to see if she could make him laugh. And she could. She'd put on Deborah's hat, the wide-brimmed one with the silk flowers, and her ankle-laced shoes and her blue taffeta dress and prance around the room like a princess. She'd sing, too, mimicking a voice that must have resembled Jenny Lind's. She made Vida sick; she made her green with envy. Vida couldn't deny that. But Leah wouldn't feel guilty about anything. She would be proud of her drunkenness, a fallen woman. And there was a part missing in Leah. She thrust herself out and everybody back, and she was never wrong. She jutted out her bony jaw and went on, empty as a scarecrow in skirts. She had thrust her way with a Bible, and now she would thrust her way with a whiskey bottle. But Vida had to admire her sister a little. Leah overcame tedium and all such-like—it was sure she hadn't cooked a pot of beans in ten years—and she made a high drama of death and how to overcome it, of wickedness and how to fall into it, of making life fly when her man was stalled in the Pool Hall and then stopped dead on the railroad tracks.

The young couples didn't return to the table, but stayed at the juke box while the record changed. It was another one of those whiny songs with the steel guitar swooning like a dying boar. Vida giggled at the thought of herself as a wallflower. She knew she could get up and ask any one of the single men to dance. But that wasn't her style, a passed-out husband or not. And Jake was beginning to worry her. What if he went to work with a hangover, groggy and fumble-fingers, and set mine timbers sloppy and the roof fell, or was too slow for the motorman and got his hands cut off, or a foot? What if he didn't show up at work for days on end and got himself fired? What if he drank up all the house money and there was nothing coming in? He hadn't enough years in the mines to retire, and way too young for Social Security. She had Betsy, her milk cow, the hens, the garden, but nothing to keep them through a winter, much less a year, or years. She was suddenly angry that she had to depend on a man, particularly since she worked her ass off from daylight to dark, harder than Jake, she figured, because she knew what a slacker he was, yet without him she and the slew of children straggling through her house would starve. *Damn men! Damn men to hell!* She had just given up her Matthew dream, and she couldn't believe, now, that she had ever thought such a thing—of course Matthew wasn't Franklin's father, and of course she was playing house like a nine-year-old when she was practically a grown woman at fifteen, pretending that Matthew was her husband and

150

Franklin their baby—god dammit, how could people be so stupid!? And now she couldn't depend on a man in the daylight hours. She had to do her part to shape Jake up. But what? She couldn't nag, bitch, whine, cajole, whimper and weep. That would work about as well as spooning alum in a bowl of biscuit dough. To hell with it. Maybe she would get drunk, too.

Chapter 7

Luke, from behind a tree, wiped his nose on his already snail-slick forearm and grabbed at Keith, accidentally
tearing his shirt pocket. Both paused in their game of tag
and looked toward the porch, wondering if Vida had heard
the loud rip. Keith put his hand over his heart in an effort
to hide the flapping pocket. Sally, standing alone under
the maple tree, and angry because the boys ignored her,
stopped picking at the scab on her elbow and waited for
her grandmother's fury to descend. Vida glanced up, but
being distracted, she merely glowered at Luke and turned
back to Ruby and William, who were quarreling, or at least
William was. Ruby's point of view was more like mud
which William's argument bogged down in. As far as Vida
was concerned, her niece didn't know her ass from a hole
in the ground, or what side her bread was buttered on.

"Of course we'll take Keith with us!" William sputtered. "Do you think I'd leave my own son behind?"

"You did before," said Ruby. "You left us both."

"That was before. Things are different, now."

"I agree with that," Vida broke in. "It ain't like it used to be. The war's over. People can get back to normal."

"William's still in the Army," said Ruby.

"Lord, yes," said Vida impatiently, "and he'll provide all the better for it. And there won't be a mine bucket to pack, bath water to heat and bank clothes to scrub."

Ruby looked away. She stared at Vida's lawn, at the morning glories by the gate, at the millet along the dusty road, the trumpet flowers and poison ivy on the fence.

"Looks like it's going to rain," she said.

"What's that got to do with the price of tea in China?" said Vida.

"Nothing, except me and William might take a walk before it comes."

"Well," Vida huffed. "I hope he can talk some sense into your head."

Vida watched them cross the yard and open the gate. She had her misgivings about Ruby going to California with William, and with Keith of course, but what were the alternatives? Ruby had lost her job at the hotel—that's what love did for the daily bread—and without a paycheck who was going to carry salt in at Deborah's, flour and corn meal and beans, not to mention bacon and porkchops?

153

How was Ruby going to feed herself and Keith? She wasn't shiftless, but she didn't have any foresight. She never planned ahead. The minute William mentioned taking her away she should have packed her bags, grabbed Keith, and headed for the Brouseks' in Coalton. They would have seen to it that William took her and Keith to California, and seen to their getting back, if need be. But no. Ruby was wishy-washy. One minute a maybe, and the next minute a maybe all over again. Vida could see how hard it would be for Ruby to leave the family. She was into it up to her neck. William would have to drag her out with a logging chain, but if Ruby kept up her dilly-dallying, soon enough there wouldn't be a William to drag her anywhere. Vida went into the house, going from room to room closing windows. She spied Pete in the kitchen. "Pete!" she shouted. "You got that strained look on your face. Run for the potty. Hurry!"

A wind was stirring the maples as Ruby and William crossed the yard. Ruby looked up, exhilarated by the contrast between the piled, dark clouds and the blue sky, by the tossing of the upper branches, the underside of the leaves palely vivid when they were turned to the sun. She shivered in the July heat as she listened to the high, rustling hiss of the leaves in the wind. Keith, watching his parents cross the road, did not ask them where they were going. His father had told him not to be such a momma's boy, and his mother's answers were always vague. He plucked at the pocket hanging loose on his shirt, wishing that he were up the road with his Great-granny. And, as if picking at his shirt were her cue, Vida hollered at him and Luke from the porch, threatening them with death itself if they ever played rough again. Sally smiled, stuck out her tongue at them, and trotted over to her grandmother.

William helped Ruby across a sag in the fence and into the pasture. He was balked, and doubly insistent because he wasn't getting his way, angry because she seesawed and kept him in suspense. They walked toward the shed which Jake and Vida used for their animals. The pasture appeared to undulate in great swaths of bottle-green and eerie viridian as the clouds moved swiftly overhead.

"I don't get it," said William. "I come back, willing to pick up where we left off, and you act like you don't want to go."

"It's not that I don't want to, but California is so far away."

"Any place is far away if you've lived up a hollow long enough."

"How am I to know you won't go off and leave us again?" asked Ruby, shuddering at the thought of the burning desert, of the vast Pacific Ocean, of living near it without any family nearby, no friends, no bus money for her and Keith to get back home on.

"I told you I was settled down, now."

"But what about last time?" asked Ruby.

"That was different. I couldn't be a coal miner."

"You didn't even let us know where you were," said Ruby, not so much complaining as stating a fact.

"I was pissed off."

"Who at?" she asked.

"I don't know. Dad, the mines, everybody."

"And what if you get mad again and leave us stranded out there?"

"I told you I won't!"

"Maybe we better go back," said Ruby, listening to the thunder rumbling over the mountains.

"No! I want to know if you're going or not. I want to get this settled. I only have four days."

Keith had been standing at Vida's fence, watching his parents stroll across the pasture. As they turned back toward him, he noticed a strange man coming up the road. The man, seeing Ruby and William in the pasture, hesitated as if to turn back; but, aware that the couple looked in his direction, he came on, striding as if he had several miles to go. Ruby, now that she had William to compare Ralph to, saw him as a fat, slouchy hound with a furtive look after being shouted at, with guilt in its eyes as it flopped on its haunch and licked its genitals. The three adults more or less crossed paths in front of Vida's.

"Howdy, you all," said Ralph, passing so close he felt obliged to speak.

"Hello, Ralph," replied Ruby in a constrained voice.

"I hear your Grandma Deborah ain't doing so good."

"She's getting pretty weak," said Ruby.

"I thought I'd look in on her."

"She'd appreciate it."

"I'd better hurry up. Looks like it's going to pour."

"Who was that!?" William demanded when Ralph had gotten up the road.

"A friend of Vida's and Jake's. He's on Jake's shift, I think. They're drinking buddies."

"Is he a friend of yours?" asked William, sneering, as they crossed the fence.

"No," Ruby answered. "I hardly know the man."

"Nobody keeping you here?"

"No, William. Good lord."

"Well, then, are you coming or aren't you?"

"To tell you the truth, William, I don't think I am."

William stopped in the middle of the road, dumfounded at last with the truth. His first impulse was to smack her very hard across the face, but seeing Keith by the gate, he merely accused her of adultery with Ralph, or some man, any man. Keith tensed as he heard his father's voice rise. A smattering of raindrops fell on his shoulders and he trembled. The thunder was louder, and the interior of the black clouds flickered gray-white with the lightning.

"William," said Ruby, "it's you been gone four years."

"You were never home when I was here! It's that god
damned family of yours, you running with them when you
should have been home with me and the kid."

"His name's Keith," said Ruby.

"I know what his fucking name is! I'm asking you for
the last time. Are you coming or not?"

"No."

"Well, I'll tell you right now, bitch, no Dingesses or
Hapneys are going to raise my son. I'm taking him."

"Take him? You by yourself in the Army, I'd like to
know how."

"I'll get a lawyer on your ass so quick you won't know
what happened."

"William, you're talking crazy! How you going to do
that? You're leaving."

"Margie will take care of it," he said.

"Your sister Margie?"

"Yeah. She's already said how sorry she feels for him,
how he needs a home."

"He's got a home!"

"Whose? That dying woman up the hollow? It's sure
not you, and do you think I'd leave him with Vida?"

"Ain't nothing wrong with Aunt Vida! And who are you
to be so concerned when you went off without a word?
How come the big change, when you ain't paid more than
ten minutes' attention to him the whole time you been
here?"

"I paid enough to see you don't give a shit what happens to him!"

"The fuck you did," she said quietly and turned away.

They were soaked by this time, and when William slapped her on the back of the head, she staggered and fell in the muddy road. Keith yelled and ran to her. The lightning was closer, now, terrifyingly white, and the thunder bellowed. He could feel it throbbing in his chest as it struck.

"Run home to Granny!" Ruby screamed to him as William dragged her upright.

Keith bolted up the road, shrieking as the black clouds yellowed with lightning and the thunder fell like a tin roof wide as the sky. Vida, who had come to yank Sally and Luke off the porch and into the house, saw Ruby and William at the gate. She dragged the children inside and grabbed Jake's double-barrel 20-gauge shotgun out of the gun cabinet. Ruby had staggered to the gate, but each time she tried to open it William snatched her hands away. Vida strode out in the drenching rain and fired once over their heads. She was so angry she hardly noticed the painful kick against her shoulder.

"Let go of her, you son-of-a-bitch!" she shouted, "or I'll blow your face clear back to Coalton!"

William looked into the yard, thinking that he had heard a different kind of thunder, sharper, less powerful, and while he was taking in the figure of Vida, Ruby managed to open the gate and slip inside. When William started after her, Vida advanced.

"One step and it'll be your last!" she yelled.

"Shit! You wouldn't—"

"Just try it. No court in hell will convict me if you pass that gate. I'd like to kill your ass, anyway, just for the fun of it. Get in the house, Ruby, god dammit! Don't just stand there like an idiot. Now, you go on down the road, William, just go back to where you come from, back to your own people, and leave Ruby in peace."

"I'll be back!" he shouted, shaking his fist. "And with the law, next time."

"We ain't scared of you or the law, either."

"I'll be taking Keith with me, you wait and see. When the lawyers get through with Ruby, there won't be a name strong enough to call her, except maybe slut."

"Keep it up, William, and you won't have a mouth to talk with."

"You wait and see!" he yelled and stomped a few yards down the muddy road. He stopped and looked back.

Vida fired over his head and he ran.

"Turd," she spat, and turned back to the house.

Both women were drenched and shivering, though Vida, as she stomped onto the porch, was trembling more from rage than the cold rain. Ruby's thin cotton dress clung wetly, voluptuously to her young body like a second skin.

"The bastard!" Vida railed. "What family does he think he's from, the dumb polack! Sally! Luke! Get your faces off the window, you look like freaks! For Christ sakes, what a time for Jake to go fishing. Fishing for a twat in a tavern, most likely. God, Ruby, look at you! Like a cat in a rain barrel. Damn! You should of told Keith to come in the house. He'll be drowned by the time he gets to Mother's. Let's get inside and dry off."

Vida pulled out the empty shells and replaced the gun in the cabinet. Luke asked for the shells; he sniffed them, stuck his fingers in them, clicked them together like puppets. Vida grabbed a towel, and in the kitchen, dried Ruby's wet hair and neck. Ruby was shivering, and Vida chaffed her arms and hands. Sally wanted to comb Ruby's pretty hair. Pete dragged his potty into the kitchen for everyone to look inside. Ruby began to cry.

"Scram, dammit!" Vida shouted at the kids. "In the living room, all of you, and don't go on the porch. The lightning will get you."

The children scattered. Vida poured coffee for herself and Ruby.

"See?" said Ruby. "See why I told you I didn't want to go?"

"All right, all right," said Vida. "He's a god-damned dog. I was wrong about him. Jesus. I see red when a man hits a woman. I was in a hair of killing him."

Ruby wiped her eyes. "That stupid Ralph," she said.

"Ralph?"

"He was coming up the road," said Ruby.

"The son-of-a-bitch," said Vida, reaching under the sink for her private pint of whiskey, an ounce which she poured in their cups. "Drink this, you're shivering."

"I'm okay," said Ruby. "I've been a fool. William wasn't worth my job. Do you think he'll take Keith?"

"Hell, no," said Vida. "What would he do with him?"

"He would take him out of spite."

"He's a jackass," said Vida, "but I don't think he'd go through the trouble. He never gave Keith a second thought."

"I better go see about him," said Ruby.

"I suppose you should, as soon as the rain slacks off," said Vida. "Don't mention any of this to Mother."

"Don't worry."

Vida frowned. "Ruby," she asked, "have you been using protection?"

"Can you get a man to?" she answered, and then she giggled. "Who thinks about that at the time, anyway."

Vida sighed and combed Ruby's pretty hair.

The storm had passed over; the sky was clearing in the west. Vida watched her niece hurry through the gate and up the road. She thought it was no wonder that the men were crazy about her. The damp cotton dress she had on clung to her body like a regular siren's, showing her firm, high titties, her little waist and the sort of low-slung, tight butt and solid thighs that make a man drool. Vida was proud of her in that regard, but lord what a fool the woman was for love. She didn't give any more thought to tomorrow than a grasshopper. And what would happen to Keith? A man couldn't take care of a child. Men liked responsibilities that had a finish to them, an edge, a clear outline they could see and back off from. Kids were fuzzy; they gathered wool in your mind and they drove you crazy; they never left your thoughts, and neither did the care or worry, or the rare times they made you laugh and think that raising them was worthwhile. Vida went inside and found Pete playing with the doo in his pot.

* * * * * * * *

The rain slackened a little; the lightning and thunder moved over the mountains and sounded distant. Keith slowed to a jog-trot, and then to a walk. The rain, when it first fell on him at Vida's, was shivery cold, and the lightning terrified him, but as he ran the storm turned invigorating, as if it were washing him, as if it were a watery door he'd broken through, leaving behind his nightmare father down the road. But he was exhausted, and the rain, now slow and steady, was once again cold on his shoulder. Water trickled down the back of his neck. He shivered and his teeth chattered. "Aie!" he shrieked as an arm

163

reached through the branches of a redbud tree and dragged him under the dripping leaves.

"Hush up, boy," Ralph growled. "You'd think somebody was trying to cut your throat."

"Ohhh," Keith shuddered. "You scared me."

"I did, did I?" Ralph chuckled. "Well, you ain't hurt, none, except you're all wet. I stopped under here when the storm broke, but it didn't help much. What was that noise I heard down there?"

"They was quarreling," Keith answered evasively.

"I mean, was that gunshots I heard?"

"I never heard no gun."

"Sounded like one to me," said Ralph. "Lord, you're shaking like a leaf. You ain't scared of me, are you? I'm a friend of your Mommy's. Here, let's set down on this rock. I was going to visit Mrs. Waugh."

"What you going up there for? Great-granny don't need no help. Franklin's with her."

"I wasn't going to help. I was just going to visit," said Ralph, wondering himself why he chanced a trip up the hollow. Everybody knew Ruby's husband was in on furlough. "What was they quarreling about?"

"My Daddy wants to take us to California."

"You all going?" asked Ralph.

"I don't know," Keith answered miserably.

"Can't you stop trembling?" asked Ralph, pulling the boy to him and rubbing his arms. "You're shaking like a dog shitting peach seeds."

Ralph sat down and hauled the boy between his legs, turning him backward as he did so. He hugged him close from behind, his chest and arms like a blanket and his chin next to Keith's ear. Keith warmed to his body heat, and stopped shaking.

"You feeling better?" Ralph asked.

"Sure am," Keith answered, relaxing. "You think my Mommy'll be okay?"

"As long as her Aunt Vida's around, I imagine she'll be all right. Vida's harder than nails."

"I just wish Great-granny wasn't sick," Keith sighed, leaning comfortably back.

"I don't know about that, now," said Ralph, "but the rain's slacking down. Almost over."

"The lightning was scary."

"There ain't no need being scared of a little lightning."

They were silent and peaceful. Keith watched the glazed leaves flutter and dip in the rain. He heard the creek, and wondered if his dam had washed away. And Ralph, though he had started up the hollow with nothing in his mind but an itchy longing, had learned from the boy that Ruby, most likely, would be around for awhile. With a mind as dense as a salt lick, he felt Keith's body pressing against his crotch.

"I'm getting a boner, "he whispered.

"A what?"

"You know, a hard-on. My dick's getting hard."

"Oh."

"You want to look at it?"

"Sure," said Keith, pulling away from Ralph and turning around.

Ralph shifted forward on the rock and unzipped himself. Keith saw what was like his own, white and round and with puckered skin on the end of it, only Ralph's was much larger. The wrinkled, pouched skin began to stretch, and out of it came an angry, red knot, vividly pink-purple, as if Ralph's insides had broken through. Keith was fascinated; it took him a moment to realize that the knot was the same as the head of his own, but ugly and painful looking.

"Does it hurt?" he asked.

"No, it don't hurt," Ralph answered, fondling himself. "It feels good, flogging your dong."

Keith got bored after a while with what he took to be Ralph's scratching and digging, and when the man started beating at himself and panting, and reaching out to Keith as if to take him by the arm, he broke away from the underbrush, scared of the man whipping at himself so much, and ran on home. On the steep path up to the house he slowed to a walk, fearful whether his great-grandmother were asleep or dead, since he knew what it

166

meant after poking at a dead cat for three days. Franklin told him that the cat would never wake up again, never. "Why not?" asked Keith. "Because it's dead," Franklin answered, scooping up the cat with a shovel and dropping it in the hole he'd dug. Keith realized, then, that Franklin was not the loony people said he was. He never talked faster than Keith could understand. He was never mean, and the fits he threw weren't his fault. All he did, anyway, was go stiff, fall down, kick at the floor and slobber a little. He always woke up.

"Franklin!" he called from the bottom of the steps.

"What?" Franklin answered, coming to the screen door.

"Is Great-granny asleep?"

"Yes. Or she was till you hollered."

"She's not dead, is she? She's just asleep?"

"That's right. Sleeping."

"Good," Keith sighed, coming onto the porch. "Lord, Franklin, you wouldn't believe what a storm."

"I seen it," said Franklin, who wasn't too friendly, since Keith at been at Jake's with his Mommy and Daddy, and playing with the kids down there. "You're wet. Best change clothes."

Slipping off his wet shirt and pants in the bedroom, he asked, "Franklin, you ever flog your dong?"

"Huh?"

"That's what that fellow, Ralph, called it."

167

"What?"

"You know," said Keith making a jerking movement with his hand at his groin.

"Sure," Franklin answered. "Who don't? I got to tie tomatoes. Rain bent them."

Keith finished dressing and rushed to his great-grandmother's room, climbing onto her bed. She was asleep, her breath so shallow he sighed as if to catch his own. The faint, sweet odor of talcum powder and the stale air in the room made him sneeze. She stirred slightly, and her eyelids fluttered.

"Is that you, Franklin?" she asked, her hand groping along the bed toward his. She found his hand and cupped it.

"Great-granny, you know it's me," said Keith.

"You ain't climbed on this bed in twenty years," she said faintly. "Even longer than that. You and Vida used to pile up in here, tickling and giggling when James was gone. But I'd have none of it, not with another woman's child drug in by James like an alley cat. But Jesus rescued me. He led you down the years so I could talk to you. Oh, poor child, can you ever forgive me?"

"Great-granny, I'm no child," said Keith, jerking his hand out of hers. "I'm six years old and you know it."

"I know how old you are, child. I counted back. You was born in April—"

"I was not! My birthday's in January!"

"April. Franklin, I reckon I ought to know. You wasn't but a month when James brought you home. April. The roses were starting to bud."

"Who's James?" Keith wailed in frustration. "And my name ain't Franklin. It's Keith."

"You don't know your own Daddy James, the whore-monger?"

"My Daddy's name is William, and mine's Keith."

"Keith? Who?"

"Keith! Keith!"

"Oh," said Deborah sharply, coming to herself. "Keith, darling, I'm sorry. I thought you was down at Vida's."

The boy figured that the old woman must have had a dream. It was easy enough to get things mixed up in a dream. He had dreamed of broad-winged hawks awhile back, and eagles, too, just last night. Franklin had to wake him up, he was hollering so much and thrashing about. But he was eager to tell her about the storm.

"I was down at Vida's, Great-granny. There was a awful storm. I was in the middle of lightning—"

"Your hair's wet, angel," Deborah said, reaching to stroke his hair.

"That's what I'm saying. There was thunder and—"

"I heard it, darling. It was God's voice. And you're my tow-headed angel. God sent you here to make it all up for Franklin."

"Ain't nothing wrong with—"

169

"I know, I know," said Deborah. "God told me all about it in the storm. I'll tell you what God said if you won't tell nobody else. You promise?"

"Sure, Great-granny."

"Well, God said in the storm that I didn't have to worry about Franklin anymore. He said that that's what Jesus was for, to take care of Franklin. Jesus loved him all the time I was harrying him. When I was hateful, when I ignored him and pushed him away, Jesus was there to lift him up. Jesus was in this house all the time. You know how I know that?"

"The storm?"

"Yes. And God sent an angel, too. A messenger. It was you He sent."

"Oh, Great-granny, I ain't no angel."

"Hush, now, if you want to hear the dream I had in the storm. Come here and snuggle up."

"Oh, all right."

"In my dream from God, there was a child in the house, but it was a strange child. Its eyes were white as the clouds, and its hair was white, too. But it had a lump between its shoulder blades, an ugly black one like a hunchback. Its mother was ashamed. She hid it under the bed, under the back porch, back in the closet, and wouldn't show it to anybody. When the child cried, it sounded like the rain, like a quiet rain on the roof, and when it laughed, the sun would shine and all the birds would sing in the trees. But nobody saw the child, no-body, till one day...."

Keith, stretched out beside his great-grandmother, had fallen asleep.

* * * * * * * *

Ruby, stomping up the road, splashing mud on her calves and the hem of her dress, missed Ralph by five minutes; he was ambling toward Ecco. The more she thought about being slapped around, the angrier she got. Damn William to hell, she fumed. Damn all them Brouseks to hell. Her love was spoiled, anyway, since there was too much pussy and cock. William was just like every other man. Not in the old days, though, not in the beginning when it was all sweet hugs, sweet kisses, back when she hardly noticed between his legs, or hers, except for the pleasure. She let her memory turn and sift, selecting what she wanted in the way of the past, her first love and the purity of it, to which she built a shrine and cast the rest into oblivion. In the immediacy of the present, however, she ranted and muddied her legs. The sun had returned; she sweated in the humidity of late July.

As she turned up the path, she noticed that Franklin was tying tomato plants the wind had blown to the ground. He was bent at the waist, and the side view of his thigh, stretched taut in his overalls, his firm buttocks, the muscular stretch of his arm as he reached down for a plant—the view of a strong, masculine body with the face aside—aroused her so unexpectedly that she nearly gasped.

"Franklin!" she called out. "You need a hand?"

He looked up, startled that Ruby was talking to him, and shook his head. She pulled and tugged at her dress, wringing out the hem. "I'm going to rinse my feet off in the creek," she said. "Come help me. I might fall in."

Franklin's look was so incredulous that she giggled. "Come on," she said, and he tagged along as she hurried through the johnson grass, under the dripping sassafras and redbud. At the creek, she slipped off her shoes, raised her dress to her thighs and waded in. She rinsed her legs, playing with them, her hands moving further and further upward. "Hardly any silt at all," she said. "After the storm, too, but it was only a shower. This water's clear enough to drink, but my dress is filthy. I may as well take it off." Franklin gaped as she did so, his astonishment so great that she laughed outright. "I'll bet you're dirty, too," she said, taking off her brassiere. "Why don't you clean up some?" Franklin tore at his brogans, overalls and shirt, and was standing calf-deep in water almost before she had her panties down. She fondled him, and as his penis hardened, she cupped water to wash the head of it, which swelled ruddy-pink, the veins bulging on the shaft. She sat at the edge of the bedrock, pulled him to his knees, and let him push himself inside. She leaned back on her arms, spread her legs, and watched his penis while he thrust it frantically in and out. It occurred to her vaguely that she was doing it with her uncle, but the thought was vague because Franklin was only four years older than she was, because he wasn't a man, really, but a moron, and because she was revenging herself on William.

He finished with a sighing gasp and leaned toward her. She pushed him away, not violently but forcefully, and squatted in the water to splash herself clean. As she began to dress, Franklin hurried into his clothes and stumbled away. She did, in fact, rinse the hem of her dress. The water felt sweet to her, cool on her arms, and the gritty bottom tickled the soles of her feet. She smiled, then giggled as she splashed her legs. She was a free woman; she could do as she pleased. And although doing it with Franklin hadn't led her to finish in any real way, her sex tingled and throbbed, and she anticipated a repeat at a time when she could finish. She was aware of doing wrong, of wickedness, even, but that added to the pleasure, as long as nobody found out what was happening. Ralph was bad enough, but Franklin would be the end of the rope if anyone knew. Her own uncle, but her half-uncle and probably not even that. She shivered with the delicious thought of the night. She slipped into her dress, and as she crossed the road and up the path, she made plans for rearranging the house a bit.

Franklin had returned to the tomato plants. He was tying the last row when Ruby walked up the path. He didn't speak, nor did she, but a look passed between them which signaled an understanding of secrecy. Abruptly, he thought of her as being on his side, the way Keith was, and joy seeped through him like water in a spring thaw, trickling from a snowbank into the sunlight and the green shoots, the tiny leaves unfurling in the light. When he finished the row he tucked the end of the twine into the ball, closed and pocketed his knife, and picked the largest, ripest tomato in the row. He walked to the apple tree and sat in the shade. He was thirsty, and the tomato fairly burst against his lips, it was so juicy. Seeds dribbled onto his chin and overall front. The juice made the tomato slippery and he dropped it in his lap. He made an odd sound in his throat which resembled a chuckle. He finished the tomato while blissfully rubbing his sore knees.

Chapter 8

After the incident between Franklin and Ruby at the creek, a time of peace and industry settled on the Waugh homeplace. With Deborah's permission, Ruby asked Franklin to open the big room at the back of the house. He carried the junk to the barn. The two double-bed mattresses he took outside for airing while Ruby swept and scrubbed the floors. She cleaned the windows inside and out, washed the curtains, and took a damp cloth to the bureaus and the closet. The room didn't have a dresser but a washstand, though a shaving mirror hung on the wall above it, and the small thing would have to do. She could go to Deborah's chifforobe if she wanted to primp, although she was so busy that prissing in front of a mirror hardly occurred to her. She was no longer getting a paycheck, and to make up for the loss she wanted to help as much as possible. In a short time, the house was spotless.

Deborah was delighted to have a young woman busy in the house again, almost like one of her own daughters. Vida, she thought, Vida and Franklin, though it was Ruby and Keith. And Franklin had perked up like nothing she'd ever seen before. He kept himself clean; he shaved; he cleaned and polished his brogans; he wore trousers now and then, instead of his overalls. He even smiled sometimes, not at her of course—she wouldn't expect him to—and not at anyone, really, but a slow smile spreading across his face when he wasn't looking at anything in particular. His smile eased her heart, made her believe that God had indeed come to her in the storm, that her dream of the white-haired, white-eyed baby with the black hump on its back was true, that one day a peddler had come—a dark, scary man who talked funny and who showed her the strangest things, not pots and pans, not needles, thimbles and scissors, but tiny golden pictures she couldn't make out, and crosses with rubies and pearls, and the tiniest candlesticks, all silver and gold—he smiled at the baby; he touched the black hump on its back; and, lo! the black hump split like the shell on a beetle and fell away; and in place of the shell unfolded the whitest wings, downy soft at the baby's shoulder blades, but broad and strong further out; and the baby rose from her arms, flying higher and higher till it was lost in the whitest clouds.

Deborah caught herself singing hymns under her breath, singing out loud, too, and was startled when Keith joined in. She was anxious that Ruby would never learn how to use the stove irons; she didn't want her curtains scorched, or the clothes either. Ruby did a good job at the washboard, but she was slow to take to the irons. And Keith was a help, lord! She never saw a child take hold at so early an age. They had more kindling than they could use in a year, and he carried water from the well like a bank mule. And Deborah was positively startled one morning to find Franklin using a toothbrush. He had always picked his teeth with a whittled matchstick, and she wondered where in the world he ever got a toothbrush. And his hair! When did he get his hair cut, and who did it? She suspected Ruby, but any thought of that she pushed from her mind.

It was time to can, and Deborah was amazed at how ignorant Ruby was. She didn't know how to plait onion tops for hanging on the back porch, or to use the darning needle and twine for draping green beans to dry on nails behind the stove. Leather britches were good in the dead of winter. She didn't know how to string and break beans properly, how to parboil tomatoes to remove the skin, how to cut corn from the cob so as not to waste the kernels, how a person had to shuck the purple hull peas before they were edible, Mercy. Didn't Leah teach her anything? She didn't know how to can, not knowing that the jars needed scalding before they were used, or how much to blanch the vegetables, or how to tighten the lids just right before putting the jars in the pot to boil, or afterwards to tap the lids for their ringing sound. But Ruby worked; she sweated alongside Franklin. The Kentucky wonders got put up, the sweet corn, the cucumbers pickled, the cabbage shredded and salted down for kraut. And they must have canned twenty quarts of blackberries. Vida was good to help; she brought salt and sugar from Barker's Store, canning lids, soda, lime and alum. The pantry was beginning to fill. The cellar house could hold the potatoes and late squash; the apples they could slice for drying in the attic. The chickens would do for meat, but what they really needed was a hog for butchering in the fall. Deborah liked ham, smoked or brined. And they needed a cow.

Vida watched the whole business in amazement. She had put up a few quarts of berries—the kids liked cobblers at Thanksgiving and Christmas—she made some grape jelly and strawberry jam, too, since Jake like them, but she didn't can much. She bought at the store. She seldom churned, since the kids drank the milk faster than she could squeeze it out of Betsy. And of course Ruby never lifted a finger along that line in her life. Vida watched them scurrying about. Keith hustled, too. She couldn't get Luke to clean his nose, and there was Keith paring carrots, or trying to. She was pleased yet jealous. Deborah was her mother, not Ruby's, and what was this sudden change of heart on her niece's part, anyway, so chummy with Franklin that a person might get suspicious. No. Ruby wouldn't do that. Forget it. Not with Franklin.

In a stunted way, Franklin still belonged to her, though like a cauterized love it ended when Franklin was a boy, a child standing at her gate. Thereafter her thoughts about Franklin were a scar, the thin tissue over a wound, a sensitive reminder of long ago. The bustle in the house sent her back to the time before the disruption in her life, before Jake, and she was saddened and angered, as if time had reversed itself and where Ruby was, she should be, not an outsider looking on, and where Keith was, Franklin should be, and not as a man carrying pecks of vegetables from the garden, but as a child who could wash tomatoes, pull the silk from the corn, who managed the simple things a child with a weak mind could. Vida snapped at Ruby a couple of times. She knew better, but she couldn't help herself.

* * * * * * *

"Come on, rise and shine!" Keith shouted, throwing himself on the bed, climbing onto Franklin and forcing his eyelids up with his fingers.

"It ain't time," complained Franklin, wrestling the boy off his chest.

"Sure it is. Look outside."

"Barely daybreak."

"Oh, come on! Mommy won't let me start a fire by myself."

"Just a second," yawned Franklin, sitting up. "You get water."

Keith raced to the kitchen, grabbed up the zinc bucket and ran outside to the well. The air was warm, and since it was August, the beginning of the dry spell, the dew was light. It hardly chilled his feet. The katydids were racketing in the weeds, and the birds, in the sumac and sapling poplars beyond the house, were carrying on so much that he wanted to laugh. The mountains were mistless, and with the morning sun yet behind them, the sky was a deep, unadulterated blue. He filled the bucket and sloshed it back to the house, where Franklin had the fire going and was cutting slab bacon.

"Here's water for the tea kettle," Keith said proudly. "Now, do you want me to get the eggs?"

"Yep."

Keith took the pail off the counter and hurried to the chicken lot. He yanked open the door to the hen house, shouted and flapped his arms, frightening the hens off their nests and into the lot. He gathered the brown, textured eggs, warm to his hand as he lifted them from the nests to the pail, and carried them cautiously back to the house. Franklin had the bacon sliced and the coffee going.

"I'll get Mommy up for the biscuits," said Keith. "She makes them better than we do."

He first tiptoed into his great-grandmother's room. She was curled up and sleeping on her side. Her shriveled body was huddled childishly under the quilt. He shuddered. But glancing at her face, at how peaceful it was, his fear vanished, and he wanted to cry. She was farther away than he had ever seen her, so distant that he had an urge to shout, to wake her up. She looked profoundly calm, as if she were in a place no one could call out to, and seemed so remote, so alone, that he was himself overcome with desolation. Tears filled his eyes, because he understood it would be mean-hearted to call to her, she was so peaceful, so likely to die, soon. His mother had told him so. He sighed heavily and went to the big room, where Ruby was sitting dejectedly on the side of the bed.

"You want to fix some biscuits, Mommy?" he asked quietly.

"In a minute, baby. I'm coming."

When he returned to the kitchen, the odor of woodsmoke made him hungry for breakfast. The coffee was perking, and though he thought the taste of it was awful, the smell meant that the day had begun. He pushed up the roll-front on the cabinet and took out flour, baking soda and lard; and, after running to the spring house for the buttermilk, he was ready for his mother to make the biscuits. But Ruby wasn't feeling well. She had to stand at the back door for a long while, sipping water instead of her usual coffee. She was able to make the biscuits, but hurried to the back porch as Franklin turned the bacon.

"You okay, Mommy?" Keith asked anxiously at the door.

"I'll be over it in a minute. You all go on and eat."

The food didn't have the savor he expected, but after they cleared the table Ruby came indoors, feeling better.

"Is the old woman going to eat?" Franklin asked.

"I'll fix her some Campbell's soup after while. Lord, you all get out of bed too early! This is worse than when I worked at the hotel."

"Me and Franklin's going to pick some corn and beans. Great-granny says we can take them down to Barker's Store."

"Clear down to the hard-road?"

"We're going to sell four bushels," said Keith. "We're taking them in the wagon."

"My goodness. You're not going to let him cheat you, are you?"

"Nah. Great-granny said Mr. Barker was honest as...well...honest as something. Franklin takes produce down there all the time."

Keith liked the word, *produce*. He knew more words than Franklin did, but that didn't matter.

"We'll ask Granny if she needs anything," said Ruby. "And you wear a long-sleeved shirt in the garden. That corn will tear you up, and beans raise welts really bad."

"Ah, shoot," said Keith.

They took the baskets off the back porch and the coaster wagon from the barn. Keith pulled the wagon, a child's toy but a big one, bright red, with slats on the sides. It was Franklin's, and he used it for hauling sacks of flour, cornmeal and grain up the road. They disappeared in the tall corn, Keith picking beans and corn below Franklin's chest, and Franklin getting those above, an easy job in the morning coolness, though dragging the baskets down the rows was a chore for Keith, and he finally asked Franklin to do it. Ruby was sitting on the front porch when they pulled the loaded wagon up to the path.

"Keith, honey, I want you to wear your shoes. You've stubbed your toes enough this summer."

"Ah, Mommy!"

"Go on, now, and put them on, or you can't go."

"Oh, all right," he said, hurrying into the house.

Ruby watched them as they eased the wagon down the path. "Don't forget the baking soda!" she shouted to them, "and try to get some bananas if you can." Keith waved and they turned the wagon onto the road and started off. Ruby saw them disappear around the curve, thinking that it couldn't be Franklin who made her pregnant. There wasn't time enough, or she didn't think there was, so it had to be Ralph or William, or one of the men at the hotel. She sighed and shifted her weight in the rocker, the nausea of morning sickness passing over her again, and a passive despair, too, since she was jobless *and* pregnant. She reached into her pocket and once again took out the lawyer's letter, opening and reading, trying to comprehend its meaning. Was she to appear in court? Was she to lose Keith? In the back of her mind she knew that she would be absolved for letting him go—how could she fight the law?—and if nothing else, she was thankful that Keith was going to William's sister, since she was a good woman and would take care of him, though Leah and the others screamed and hollered about William, the troublemaking hunky who deserted her and Keith for the Army, and as much as deserted her again by reenlisting, and then shoving divorce papers in her face on top of that. An unfit mother, huh! That was calling the kettle black. But she couldn't go to Ford Ord. She went to Ohio once, up to Dayton, and the city made her very uneasy, so the idea of California, even the mention of it, filled her with dread. There was a bustle about the outside world that drained the life out of her, made her feel like a nobody, people looking at her with no more regard than they'd give a fire hydrant.

And the actual living with William, as she remembered it, was boring. She had to admit the truth. Boring. He was like a Greyhound bus driver on a bad road in a snowstorm, tense and staring up ahead, and it didn't matter if he was at the table or in the living room or in bed, especially in bed after they set up house. He couldn't relax and have a good time. He had his eyes on a goal up there in the future, whatever in god's name that was, and treated her more often than not like a passenger who wasn't worth the ticket she laid her money out for. And farthest back in her mind was the fact that she didn't want to leave Charles and Della, Jake and Vida and the rest of the family, not even Leah. It was one thing to love William but another to live with him. He was strict and mean, really mean. He had a jealous streak a mile long.

Not like Franklin. It was fun to tease him. He was always hard, and she liked holding him off, dallying with him, teaching him how to kiss and where to caress her, and he was so sensitive that just to touch him was a joy; he shivered and trembled and never got enough. He was like a teenage boy, not a grown man, and he never told her to do anything, never bossed her or sneered at her, or said anything snide or sarcastic. From the beginning, they kept his door closed, with a chair propped in front of it, but still she was a little worried about Keith. He slept in the big bed next to hers, and sneaking to Franklin's room was a problem a few times, what with the boy finding her missing. He had called out her name. She'd hurried back to the big room, telling him that she'd gone to pee, or to get a drink of water, except for the one time when he got out of bed and saw her coming from Franklin's room. She told him she thought that Franklin was having a fit and she had gone to see about him. She smiled and giggled. Franklin was having a fit, no doubt of that.

"Ruby!" Deborah called from the bedroom, "can you come help me on the pot?"

"Coming!" Ruby shouted, knowing that her family would carry her along, take care of her somehow or another.

* * * * * * *

After walking a mile, and that only partway to Barker's Store, Keith realized the foolishness of wearing shoes, so he took them off and tucked them under the baskets. And after pulling the wagon a lot less than his share, he gladly turned the handle over to Franklin, protesting however that he must push from behind, but that too he soon gave up and took Franklin's hand, walking alongside him and chatting, aware only in the vaguest way of his mother's troubles, the letter she kept reading and reading. He was happy that she was home at night. They passed his Great-aunt Vida's, but no one was about. She must have taken Luke and Sally home. Franklin paused at the gate. Keith felt his hand tighten.

"Jake's place," said Franklin.

"Come on, now. Mommy said not to poke."

They strode on and Keith grew shier as the number of houses increased. By the time they reached the mouth of the hollow he was practically tongue-tied, so much so that at Barker's it was Franklin who dealt with the store owner. Keith could only point to the baking soda and the bananas, and then to his treats, the Redhots. Mr. Barker counted the money into Franklin's palm so carefully that Keith flushed with humiliation.

"Don't worry about where you come from, son," Mr. Barker said as he counted the change. "There's always heaven above, high above the sky. Don't worry about all the men could have been your father. Christ didn't have no earthly father. It's all woman's doing, anyhow."

A customer sniggered.

Keith hated people. He hated being down at the hard-road. But as they headed back up the hollow and the houses faded behind, as the trees and the mountains closed in, his spirits lightened, and he teased Franklin into eating a few of his Redhots, which were sweet and fiery on the tongue.

When they came to Vida's place, Franklin tightened his grip again, and at the gate he stopped. Keith could do no more than look up sideways, since he was trapped at the end of Franklin's arm. Keith's hand wasn't crushed; it wasn't even hurt, but he knew it would be impossible to pull away. Franklin went stiff-backed and began to jitter on his heels, but he didn't jerk so violently as to fall down, champ and grind his teeth, or spit and dribble on himself. Rather, with his head raised rigidly straight, and glaring directly up the road, and with his whole body vibrating like an upright wrecking bar, he began to shout in a high, rasping voice. "Cunt! Pussy! Whore! Your belly dry up like a well, fire in it, fire like hell! The Horseman get your pussy, locusts eat it! Egypt plague! Sores in your cunt, leprosy, barren hole! You hunch under a mule, suck dog's dick, hog's dick in your ass! Jake falls in the hole, Jake drowns in the hole! Drown Jake! Drown Jake! Eat by the worm! Your children the Devil's, Devil children, God damn them all to hell everlasting, forever, motherfucker!" Keith knew that Franklin's raving was nasty, but he couldn't help thinking that it sounded a little like Reverend Bledsoe's, and his Granny Leah's, too.

"Stop it! Stop it!" screamed Vida as she came running from the house. "Go home! Go on! Go!"

Franklin's fit ended almost as suddenly as it began. He relaxed his grip, and they sauntered casually on as if nothing had happened.

Vida was left standing in the yard, glaring at their backs. She nearly fainted. She felt as if she had been struck in the face several times. She staggered to the porch steps and sat down. Anguish overcame her, the sense of a wasted life, a void, as if she were falling away from the earth. She was shocked, trembling and burning far beyond rebuke of Franklin or reproach for herself, beyond hatred or blame. What had happened was a fact, a result of what she did. She had allowed Jake to refuse her son. She had wanted to live a normal life. She had wanted to think that the past was somebody else's trouble. She had wanted to get away from Deborah and Daddy James. Jake offered her freedom. She took it, and now the past opened before her its baleful eyes of the inevitable. Nothing would change the past, or alter it. She had to accept that she had failed Franklin. She had turned away from his need, a need which she herself created. Forgiveness wasn't even an issue. She destroyed Franklin's life as surely as laying a shotgun to his head. By watching him being driven from the gate she could as well have pushed him over a cliff, high on the mountains where it seemed to her eternity dwelt, while she and everyone in the hollows and by the river were leaves in the wind, falling leaves, weeds and grasses along the creek which shriveled and died in the frost. How could she go on? How could she live but bluff it through? To go on screaming at kids, wiping their asses, feeding them oatmeal, yanking a husband straight by letting him be, by showing him a path that led to self-respect, which was his to go on or not. She could make her own way, with him or without him, since the wind on the mountains sighed, far-distant, and it said without a voice: *live, die, I will pass over anyway, forever.* She grieved for a long while, then dogtrotted up the hollow. Franklin must never behave that way with Jake in the house.

* * * * * * * *

It seemed to Franklin as if a heavy burden, which had bunched and cramped his shoulders, had dropped away like a sack of coal he'd dug out of the hill. He hummed to himself and smiled, pushing his lank, black hair off his forehead. Keith was quiet, but happy also, and put his arm around Franklin's waist.

"Phew, Franklin, you stink," he said, grimacing. "Let's me and you go to the creek after dinner."

"Nope."

"Why not?"

"Don't want to."

"Oh, come on. You can help me with my dam."

"All right," Franklin relented. "I'll help with that."

Keith's heart was further lightened, on coming up the path, to see Deborah on the porch. She smiled and waved to them, and Ruby came to the screen door when Keith shouted that Barker's had bananas. Franklin ducked to the back, and Keith, coming onto the porch and seeing his great-grandmother bundled in a quilt, realized just how hot he was, and sweaty. And looking out from the porch to the sloping yard, the road and the mountains, he saw them yellowed with sunlight, a dusty dry-hot yellow, and he was thirsty; it seemed that his whole body was thirsty. He was sure, also, when he handed Deborah the bananas and kissed her on the cheek, that he wouldn't tell her what happened at Vida's gate.

"You're a sweet thing, Keith," murmured Deborah, "to think of a old woman."

"Mommy told me," he said, pleased nonetheless with himself for remembering the fruit.

"Well, thank both of you. I don't know what me and Franklin would do right now without you and Ruby."

Keith beamed. "Ah, Great-granny. Me and Franklin had fun." He skipped indoors, hungry for lunch, and thirsty. He and Franklin ate cold corn bread and washed it down with buttermilk. "We're going to work on my dam, now, Mommy," he said, wiping his mouth with the back of his hand.

"Take a rag and soap," she said. "That way I won't have to worry about your bath. I want you to wash your ears, good, and if you don't get them clean, I will."

"Shoot. I'll do it."

He and Franklin waded through the tall dusty grasses and weeds alongside the road, made their way through the underbrush and came to the sun-flecked shade under the trees. They paused, and a hush fell over them for a moment. Keith looked back. Through the deep green shade of the branches he saw the road as a gold stripe or slash. He imagined people scurrying along, as at Ecco, shouting and pointing, tugging and shoving one another, all of them going somewhere. It hurt his eyes; it excited and depressed him. He turned away and they tread through the ground ivy, moss and fern, and Keith's spirits lightened when they came to the sunny bedrock. He stripped to his shorts and waded in, whooping as the cold water reached his knees. "Come on, Franklin, you promised!" he shouted, and Franklin hesitantly took off his brogans, rolled up his overalls and followed after Keith. They worked on the dam and were gratified to see the water rise along the outcrop. "Now we got to take a bath," Keith announced.

"You got to, not me," said Franklin.

"You do, too, so come on."

Franklin undressed to his shorts and squatted in the water, allowing Keith to wash him down, luxuriating in the sudsy scouring. He tingled with pleasure. Keith pushed when he finished scrubbing, and Franklin fell backward, squawking and laughing, into the water. It was the first time Keith had heard him laugh, and thought that the sound was funny, like a mixed-up rooster's crow and a screech owl. Keith began to giggle, and he squealed as Franklin splashed him. Deborah and Ruby heard them from the porch, and Deborah smiled.

"They're both children," she commented, and then asked, "Do you think they'll take Keith away?"

"I suppose they will," said Ruby, who was beginning to think of Franklin as a man more than a retard now that she was pregnant, and she kept asking herself: just how dumb was he, anyway? "Nothing I can do," she said, "with what William's holding on me."

"You oughtn't got pregnant."

"And the moon oughtn't shine, I guess. But William don't know I'm pregnant. It's the witnesses I'm talking about he's got lined up."

"Just like a man, as if a woman could get in trouble by herself. They're a case, ain't they, men are, always flying off somewhere, and us only brood hens for all our pluming ourselves. We don't fly. We just peck at the grain and lay eggs."

"Well, my bird sure flew the coop," said Ruby, chuckling.

"My James never did. He brought a cuckoo to the nest."

"Granny!" said Ruby, laughing despite herself. "You cut that out."

"Keith's made it easier. You know how I hate and despise that sick-calf look on Franklin's face. It's gone, now, and Keith's to thank for it."

Ruby knew who else was to thank for it, but she said, "You making over Keith the way you do, it's a wonder Franklin ain't jealous."

"Keith's the only thing he's ever had," said Deborah. "I never loved him."

"Granny, you blame yourself too much. I told you that before."

"I didn't," said Deborah softly. "Never, but Vida did."

"Was Jake all that set against taking Franklin?" Ruby asked.

"We didn't really know till afterwards. In my heart I never really thought he would. I convinced her to marry, but not for her sake. In my heart I did it out of cruelty. I did it to spite Franklin."

"That don't matter," said Ruby. "Not now, anyway. Aunt Vida's marriage turned out good enough."

"That's true. Hers is a good marriage, sin on my heart or not. It's like that, now, with Keith. He's lifting the sin off my heart. He's carrying it like an angel a little more ever day, and he turns it from the raven to the dove. He's like a bridge from me to Franklin, and Franklin can't be jealous of a bridge that love walks on."

"He's just a boy, Granny, and believe me, he's no angel."

"You can't see what I see," said Deborah.

"No, but I can see where Mommy got her preaching talent at."

"That may be, but Leah never took to me like she did to James. Oh, I've talked myself plumb tired. I haven't been this gabby for a week."

"I'm glad you're up and about. You're looking better."

"I feel some better," she sighed.

Keith and Franklin wrung out their underwear, shook the water off themselves, and stood in the sun to dry. They dressed and were leaving the creek when Franklin clamped his hand on Keith's shoulder and whispered to him to hush. Keith saw, then, his Great-aunt Vida striding up the road, a twisted look on her face. They crouched in the underbrush until she passed, then slunk back to the creek to hide. From the porch, Deborah and Ruby watched her hurry up the path, and they could tell by the way her head was thrust forward, by the way her feet struck the ground, that trouble was coming. Vida stormed onto the porch and stood with her hands on her hips, her forehead beaded with sweat. She glowered at Deborah.

"God-dammit, Mother!" she shouted. "I told you before to keep your eye on Franklin. He's going to end up in the asylum!"

"He don't need no feeble-minded hospital," said Deborah. "We can take care of him."

"Sure you can! Letting him run loose on the road like that. He threw a fit in front of my house, and I never heard such filth in my life, and god knows I've heard my

194

share. You remember he tried to kill me with that ax! Jesus Christ, you can't have him running up and down the road. I warned you that Jake was threatening to get papers on him from Weston."

"Don't do that, Vida, not till I'm dead," said Deborah weakly.

"Shit, Mother, you ain't going to die. You got years ahead of you, yet. I'm talking about Franklin."

"I ain't got days ahead of me, and you know it. You're talking about when I'm dead. Wait till then, and you can make up your own mind."

"Stop it, Mother! I sometimes wonder if you're not crazier than he is."

"I would be crazy if you took my obligation away from me, what little of it I've seen to these twenty-eight years."

"He ain't no obligation. He's a menace to the public!"

"We took him, Vida! He was a baby and we took him. James could have let him die in the weeds, but he didn't. And we took him. You did! You loved him when I couldn't, and now my heart is softened, I can't harden it up again. I can't, and you can't burden your love. You can't stony up because of shame."

"Shame? What in the hell are you talking about?"

"Shame for leaving him. But it was me did that. I as much as drove you into Jake's arms."

"You did what?"

"Yes. Spite! It was all a grudge! It's not your fault. It's mine!"

"Mother," Vida whispered hoarsely, "I don't know what the fuck you're talking about. And stop shouting like that. You'll make yourself sick."

"Watch your language, daughter," responded Deborah out of habit. "It's just that Franklin's not your fault. You didn't leave him. You never did. That's why you're here, now. I didn't want you sacrificing your life for Franklin's sake, so I urged Jake on you. I did it for kindness sake out of one side of my mouth, and malice out of the other. You didn't leave him. You never did. I did. I grudged him ever day of his life. When I let him live, when I didn't smother him with the pillow like I was—"

"Granny!" exclaimed Ruby.

"Hush, child. I let him live, but only to let him suffer. I should have killed him in his baby clothes, but I was a coward, and then a disciple of the Devil. I hated him with my whole heart."

"God, Mother," Vida cried out, "if you hated anybody, you hated Daddy James!"

"Oh, god, yes! I hated him! I hated my husband!"

The old woman slumped in the rocker, sobbing with the spontaneity of a child.

"Oh, Mother, hush, hush," soothed Vida, kneeling before her, hugging her and wiping her face.

Ruby was stunned. She trembled at the thought of killing a baby. Before she moved to the big room, she had been afraid of waking in bed with her grandmother and finding her dead, which would have been horrifying and repulsive, and now was the greater fear that life itself had no foundation, that love was not as natural as blood and breath, that no one, not even herself, was safe.

Deborah had to be helped to bed, and there was supper to be seen to. Vida left directly, and Ruby busied herself in the kitchen, attempting to shake off her fear, attempting to push back the shadows that crept into her heart. She was faint and weak, and wanted to cry. Franklin and Keith came back to the house, but the happiness had left their faces. They were subdued, pensive, and ate in silence, with only the sound of their forks against the plates, the scraping up of fried potatoes, the smacking noise of their mouths.

After dinner, Ruby and Keith sat miserably on the front porch, Ruby in the rocking chair and Keith at her knees on the floor.

"Mr. Barker said Franklin didn't have no earthly father."

Ruby paused, her cigarette halfway to her lips. "What?"

"He was like Jesus," said Keith. "Come from the sky."

"Mr. Barker sounds like he's off in the head."

"I reckon," said Keith. "I don't like it down there."

Chapter 9

Deborah was dead and in her casket in the living room. Even on the porch, Ruby could smell the cloying musk of gladiolus and carnations, and a faint dusty odor related to silk and taffeta, and fainter still, an odor both astringent and suffocating. She stared at the cardboard fan in her lap, the print of miniature roses, violets and buttercups, bordered by the name, Riverton Funeral Home. The shape reminded her of a catalpa leaf. She turned it to the other side and saw blank-gray cardboard, the staples in the thin wooden handle. She was grieving for Deborah, but she was also concerned about Franklin, the man whose house she'd been living in since spring. Of course, everybody knew it as Deborah's house, but Franklin was the man in it. Ruby didn't realize that at first. She thought she was moving in with her Granny Deborah, but she was actually moving in with Franklin, whom everyone assumed was Leah and Vida's half-brother, but he was eighteen years younger than Leah, and fourteen younger than Vida. And he was only four years older than Ruby. She puzzled in her mind who Franklin's father was, and using a logic which she couldn't admit to anyone, herself included, she deduced that, since she didn't know which man had fathered the child she was carrying, Julie Beth Dickins hadn't known who fathered Franklin. She concluded that Franklin wasn't her uncle. Or half-uncle. In the recesses of her mind, where reality accommodated itself to the longed-for, she knew that Franklin couldn't be her Grandpa James's. Maybe he belonged to her Great-uncle Matthew and was only her cousin.

She had heard so much talk about Franklin, from Deborah and Vida, that she felt as if she'd known him all her life, known him even as an infant; and his disorder—his convulsions and suffering—and his isolation from everyone stirred her intensely, particularly so in that her pity was bound to him erotically, a mixture of sorrow and lovemaking which she had never experienced with a man before. Ruby was in love with Franklin. And now that Deborah was dead, he was in fact the master of the house.

Just a couple of days after talking about how she had once considered the infanticide of Franklin, Deborah asked Reverend Bledsoe and his wife witness her will. She gave Franklin the house and thirty-five acres, which was considerable. Forty acres, including the big pasture across from Jake's, she gave to Vida. Out of her savings, which she had hidden in a cubbyhole of the dresser, she withdrew her burial money and willed the rest, a little over nine hundred dollars, to Leah. Ruby was startled that Deborah had so much money, and she was impressed that the old woman could handle business, especially the undertaker whom she had asked to the house. Ruby found it hard to think about caskets—period—much less talk about buying her own, and dickering over the price, too, and the tombstone, which she was having the undertaker purchase for her, and fussing the whole time about the cost of the embalming and the service. A couple of weeks later she died in her sleep.

Ruby was sad that Deborah was dead, but the sorrow wasn't deep. She hadn't known her long enough. Ruby's living arrangements figured in as heavily as her sorrow, maybe more so, since she had to go on living but wasn't sure where, or how. Her mind kept centering on Franklin. She was shocked that others thought him seriously enough retarded to be institutionalized. He wasn't a moron or an idiot. Even if he were, she could live at the house and be his caretaker. But how without money? He couldn't work, and where could she? Not at the hotel anymore. There was nothing around for a woman, except maybe Woolworth's in Riverton, something like that, but that was too far away, and nothing around for a man, either, except the mines, and Franklin could never work in one. Why was Jake insisting on sending Franklin to the State Hospital? He kept saying that all that was needed was to have the family sign the papers. Leah said she would see him in hell, first. Did he think he would get the house and the thirty-five acres if the men in the white coats came and carried Franklin off? She said she wasn't signing shit, not till she was good and ready, and that was probably never. Keith, sitting on the floor, took the fan out of Ruby's lap and swatted at the flies.

"Where's Franklin?" she asked.

"He's out at the barn," Keith answered.

"Oh, lord," she said, and began to weep.

Keith got up and stood beside her rocker, thinking it was Deborah she was weeping for. He put his arms around her neck.

"It's all okay, Mommy," he said quietly. "Great-granny's in heaven. The preacher said so."

"I guess she is," said Ruby, wiping her eyes, wondering who in god's name was the father of the baby she was carrying. Not Franklin. Surely it wasn't Ralph. Surely to Christ it was William. She would know—boy or girl—after it was born, when she saw if its eyes were brown or blue, its hair black or blond, its skin olive-pink or rose-white. She trembled at the thought of it belonging to a stranger.

Keith was momentarily puzzled. If Deborah were in heaven, what was she doing in the living room? What part of her was in heaven? The part of her that was asleep? The coffin did look like a bed, a little one. If she was asleep, not dead like the cat, then she wouldn't rot like it did. She would wake up pretty soon to the thing itself,

Jesus and God and all the angels. A shiver ran over him. How would she get to heaven? Would Jesus dig her out and carry her away? Would she be His arms as He flew? Keith sighed and hugged his mother.

It never occurred to him that he would truly lose her if he went to his Aunt Margie's. His thought had his mother and Franklin in it. He didn't conceive of a final separation, a parting, but rather that the two were somehow included in his leaving, that they would go with him, and he would have them and his Aunt Margie, too. And what were plans, anyhow? How did the men in black suits know to come and carry his Great-granny away in her nightgown, and two days later bring her back arrayed like a queen, carrying her up the steps and into the house, setting flowers around her, and shiny candlesticks? Who told the women to bring the food? Who told the men to dig the grave? How did plans come about that he was to go to his Aunt Margie? He didn't know who she was. He couldn't remember ever seeing her, or speaking to her. Everything was a mystery to him.

Jake couldn't figure it. His wife was the last person he expected to break down, not hard-ass bristling Vida. Who would have figured so ribby a woman could have split like Moses's rock and cried two Kleenex boxes full? Jake and the men had shoved the couch back against the wall to make room for Deborah's coffin, which they had to take the door casing down for, so as to get it from the front porch into the living room, and the flowers had an odor which

202

reached back through the nose and grabbed the brain like ice tongs. Jake couldn't stand the smell, or the flies that swarmed in the house with the constant opening and closing of the screen door. He struggled through the kitchen, which was crowded with gossiping ladies who fanned themselves and the food-laden table, to keep the flies away. On the back porch, he nipped at the half-pints as they were passed around.

"Can you believe they ain't got no electricity," somebody commented to nobody in particular, "and here it is 1946."

"And some of you men will be up here all night," said Jake, "with nothing but kerosene lamps and the moon."

"You ain't staying, and you a son-in-law?" asked Wade. He twitched his shoulders, shook his arms in his sleeves. The day was hot, and when the sun broke through the clouds, he sweated in his black suit.

"You're talking like a crazy man," said Jake. "Vida will, but not me. I'm going to sleep in my own bed. I reckon you'll stay, since you and Leah are thicker than thieves lately."

"Suppose so," said Wade. "Some of these people will need a ride home after dark. I can sleep in the car."

"How's it feel hauling my sister-in-law around like she was the Queen of Sheba?" asked Jake. He was sticky and tugged at the front of his white shirt. Damned Vida. She shouldn't have put so much starch in it, and his gabardine slacks were like blankets wrapped around his legs.

"It's fine," said Wade quietly. He was thinking that if Charles were in the back yard, him being Leah's son and twenty years younger than Jake, then Jake wouldn't be shooting his mouth off so much. "I don't mind driving."

"Well, one thing," said Jake, changing the subject, "we can get that half-wit Franklin to the asylum, now. I could tell you stories about him that'd raise the hair on your head. He even tried to kill Vida, once, with an ax."

The men let their attention drift, having heard too often Jake's horror stories which had never been proved, not by Franklin's behavior as far as they could tell, and what little they did listen to left them feeling creepy, knowing that some sort of lying justification was being foisted on them, but one which, since they were Jake's buddies, they couldn't defend themselves against, as if they stood there looking at the well box while Jake dropped black widow spiders in their pants pockets. Wade had heard Jake's bullshit before, but he wasn't the kind to interfere and argue. And Jake did have a point no one could dispute, and it was that, Deborah being dead, Franklin had nobody in the world to care for him, certainly nobody on the back porch.

"Now that Mrs. Waugh has passed away," Wade commented, "I think that Ruby and Keith are going to live with Leah."

"Ruby won't last a week," said Jake. "Leah will pick at her too much, just like she does everybody."

"It was George's death got to her," said Wade, "and her quitting preaching. I think she's getting better, now, though."

"Huh," said Jake. "May be. The whiskey ought to help, since she drinks enough of it. Her old man picked a hell of a way to go, didn't he? Jesus. Getting run over by a train. Where's that half-pint I saw awhile ago?"

Leah got sick of the caterwauling inside. She went to the front porch, swishing in her flowered rayon dress back and forth in front of her daughter, touching her peroxided hair and patting at her thin neck with her lace handkerchief. Keith scurried off the porch and around the house.

"I'm glad all those little heathens are down at Vida's," said Leah. "It's rackety enough around here without them screaming kids. Reverend Bledsoe been here?"

"Yes," said Ruby. "Him and the undertaker was here this morning. Reverend Bledsoe said he might be back this evening."

"Good," said Leah. "I'll be gone by then."

"Mommy, you ain't staying the night?"

"I sure ain't," she said. "Half the hollow will be having Wade drive them home. It's not his place to haul people around like a Greyhound bus."

"I guess not," said Ruby, sighing.

"Shit. There wasn't no golden halo under her pillow that everybody has to stand guardian over her head. You'll be here, and Vida, and all the no-goods till the food is gone."

"Mommy! Somebody will hear you."

"They're all too busy hearing their own heads rattle to worry about us. I reckon Jake's determined to send Franklin off to the asylum?"

"Yes," said Ruby.

"The greedy hog," spat Leah. "He's got that bottom down there by his house when he got them acres. He thinks if he gets Franklin declared a lunatic, then him and Vida can claim everything up here. The first clod of dirt won't hit her coffin before they're inside tearing down the stovepipes and carrying off the beds."

"Don't say things like that."

"It's the truth, Ruby, and you know it. What's worse is Mother favored Vida over me, always did, and here Vida wants to snatch the house out from under her casket."

"You don't have to talk so loud."

"For a daughter of mine, Ruby, I don't know how you ended up weaker than a broom straw."

"I took it after Daddy, you said."

"That's right, after George. He's the only man I know could fall asleep in front of a train. The only one I'd want to know. Jesus. These flies."

"Well," said Ruby, "now you got a man wrapped around your little finger."

"You don't know Wade, that's all. You don't wrap him around nothing, just seems like it. I'll tell you a fact, Ruby. I ain't all that interested in the man. He hems me in. Where is he, anyhow?"

"On the back porch with the rest of the men, I guess," she said. She was hot and sweaty, and plucked at her dress. She wished that she could have a drink of whiskey.

Inside, on the couch, Vida wiped at her eyes. Unspoken, the word *never* throbbed insistently in the wound of her grief. A great part of her life had disappeared forever, and she was anguished by the emptiness. She would never again hear Deborah talk about Cain and Abraham and Moses, about Joseph and Ruth, about Mary and the baby Jesus. She would never again see her at the stove or the sink, never see her sweeping the floor or darning a shirt, never see her in the garden, or at the springhouse, or on the porch in her rocker. There was nothing, nothing, and how go on? Go on to where, and struggle for what, and why? How could anyone face that inevitability? She, too, would die. She would depart from her children, and they would die. The whole world would disappear. It would vanish into darkness. Vida felt herself becoming small, becoming a child again, a baby isolated in a cradle in the dark, awake and terrified. She cried out as an infant does, weeping and helpless against the terror of black nothingness.

Then, somehow or another, she seemed to be standing a long way off. She saw the infant alone in the cradle; she saw its suffering. A great pity overwhelmed her. She approached the baby; she touched its cheek; she bent to lift it up. There was no surprise, when looking at its face, that she saw herself and her mother, and then, not a blur but indistinct, she saw Daddy James and Matthew, Franklin and Keith, her children and grandchildren. She sighed deeply, recognizing the sorrow in them all, and saw that the cause was death. She wept again, but there was balm in the tears, and grief for life itself. She wished she had Della to talk to, but Della and Charles were babysitting.

Leah, after getting her fuss in with Ruby, headed through the house for the back porch. Keith returned to his mother's side.

What with the flowers, the women's perfume and the sweat, the living room was sickly sweet. The women fanned themselves. Leah glanced at her mother in the coffin and thought her nose looked like a shark's fin. Vida was still on the couch, her eyes watery and red, her nostrils a bright pink, her hair matted with sweat and her dress puckered at the waist and bunched at her armpits.

"You got to stop it, Vida," said Leah in a nasty voice as she passed through the room. "You can't carry on like it's the end of the world. You'll make yourself sick. And you ladies go on and get a bite of food. I imagine the men are hungry, too."

But Leah didn't stop to eat. She took a Coca-Cola out of a cooler, opened it and strolled on through. The men on the back porch bristled a little, as though a razorback were intruding on a convention of fattening hogs. They were lounging, swaybacked, bowed, splayed, slouching against the porch posts, the wall; a couple of them on the ground had a foot propped on the low porch, an elbow on a knee.

It was only Wade—tall, corpulent, lumbering Wade—who was pleased to see her. The conversation stopped.

"Wade, darling, give me a drink," she said in the worst imitation of a flirt. After chasing the whiskey with a drink of the soda pop, she added, "Well, Jake, what you all been jawing about?"

Before Jake could answer, Vida burst onto the porch, her red eyes squinted, her shoulders hunched up, her arms akimbo. Leah had yanked her away from the contemplation of death as surely as if she had grabbed her by the hair of her head, and to tell the truth, Vida was glad of it. She needed distraction. The men scrambled away as from a freak tornado. The sisters glowered at each other.

"I reckon I can grieve for my own mother!" she said.

"I can grieve well enough, too," said Leah, "but I ain't going at it like Noah's flood."

"Why is it when George got killed I took your side against Mother's throwing off on him, and now you can't let me cry in peace?"

"Your tears might wash your forty-odd acres away."

"I didn't write her will!" Vida shouted.

Leah scowled at her sister. "You been bad-mouthing me ever since I took up with Wade," she said. "Seems kind of two-faced to me, one side bawling and the other side whispering all kinds of trash."

"For Christ sakes, Leah! George ain't been dead two months and here you are already backslid—no, worse than backslid, since you was a preacher—and drinking and swarping around like a floozy, taking up with a man about half your age."

"You leave Wade out of this," said Leah. "You all are jealous because he can hang onto his money and buy himself a nice car."

"It's pink, Leah! A giant pink hog with the looks of a whore-hopper on wheels. And Wimpy Wade? I wouldn't call him a man. I'd call him hamburger grease with clothes on."

"Hah!" shouted Leah. "You're jealous because he's clean and wears a suit, which is more than you could ever say for Jake. It's the house, ain't it, some place you can stick that ribby crew of yours, them daughters and grandchildren, and land for your ramp-eating cow and Jake's sorry excuse for a horse. That's why you're carrying Franklin off to the State Hospital. You mothered him enough in the old days, and then walked off and left him."

Spectators had gathered at the door and the kitchen window. The men had fanned out in a semicircle.

"I married Jake!" shouted Vida. "I didn't walk off from nobody."

"It's funny," said Leah, "that you couldn't take the bastard home, yet Uncle Matthew hung around the place so much I wonder who Franklin belongs to."

"Meaning what?"

"I'm not one to accuse. I wasn't around at the time. I was up on Hereford Creek raising my own children, but I wasn't so far away I was blind, and twice the shame on you if what I suspect is true about the moron, and then you leaving it with Mother."

"Your preaching's done warped your mind, Leah. Franklin is Daddy James's and that Dickins girl."

"That was the story Mother told, but I think we got eyes to see and ears to hear."

"Matthew had nothing to do with it, and I sure didn't. Daddy James did."

"That's right!" shouted Leah. "Blame it all on my dead father. Blame it all on Daddy James. That's what mother did."

"You crazy thing! You think Daddy James was God, that's what your problem is. I remember you flouncing around him, flirting like the worst kind of tease, so if Franklin has a mother, you'd fit the case in the spirit of it, since George most likely was limp as a noodle from the start."

"Aggh!" screamed Leah, leaping at her sister with clawed fingers.

They were entangled on the porch in seconds, legs and arms flailing, hairpins flying, their summer dresses ripped. They cursed, squalled and yelped. Their imprecations rent the hot, August air as they fell. All the men but Wade were sniggering quietly, erotically intent on the two women rolling about, entangled and writhing on the floor.

Ruby ran through the house and onto the back porch. "Jake!" she shouted. "Grab Vida. Wade! Get over here and help me with Mommy."

As if out of a daze, the men sprang forward. Jake bent to take hold of Vida, while Wade dragged Leah back by her arms. They pulled the two women to their feet. The sisters were panting, streaks of sweat on their dusty faces, scratches on their forearms. Leah's dress was torn, revealing her brassiere, and Vida's nose bled.

"Jake, for god sakes," said Ruby, "how could you let your own wife get in a cat-fight?" She straightened the two women's clothes as best she could, tugging and patting and setting in place. She took her hankie out of her belt and dabbed at Vida's nose.

"Don't quarrel at me, Ruby," protested Jake, taken aback by her sudden forcefulness. "I didn't start it."

"No, but you could have stopped it. And you, Wade, letting my mother make an ass of herself."

"Oh, hush up, Ruby," said Leah. "I'm all right and so is Vida."

"Mommy! Wade's taking you home, right now!"

"Not till I'm good and ready," Leah huffed.

"Now! Go on, Wade, take her."

"How come you're on your high horse?" whined Jake.

"I ain't," said Ruby, "but I'll tell you this. And you, too, Mommy, and you Aunt Vida. I've lived up here all summer, and it's the closest I've come to having a home in a long time. The woman in there is dead and in her casket. My own Granny, your own Mother, and it seems to me if you want to fight you could wait till tomorrow when she's under the ground!"

Ruby burst into tears. The spectators looked at the porch floor, at the washtub hanging on a nail, the hoe leaning against the wall, anywhere but at the crying woman. Faces disappeared from the screen door and the kitchen window. Wade, as he led Leah away, thought with a great sadness that Ruby was the woman he ought to be with. It was she who needed him, not the maniac he had by the arm, who could beat her way through Armageddon with one hand, the other clutching a whiskey bottle. He sighed, knowing the impossibility of it. But his sigh was edged with excitement. Maybe Ruby would stay with Leah, and he was often at Leah's.

Keith had rushed through the house with his mother. He witnessed the fight, and when he saw Leah being helped into the car, he ran for the barn. Franklin was always at the barn when people bothered him. "Franklin, where are you?" he whispered, peering into the brown-gray recess. Without hearing an answer, he panicked for a moment, but then saw Franklin stir at the far end. He rushed forward. "There was the worst fight you ever saw!" he exclaimed. "Granny Leah and Aunt Vida was—"

"I ain't going to no loony bin," said Franklin.

"You have to," said Keith, "the same as me going to my Aunt Margie's."

"I ain't going to no funny farm."

"Oh, Franklin, you can't stay here by yourself. Ain't nobody to look after you."

"I don't need nobody!" Franklin shouted.

"You do, too."

"How come? You think I ain't twenty-eight years old? I know how old I am, and I ain't never had a fit I didn't get over. I ain't no dummy. If anybody is, it's her that's dead, and Ruby and you! You couldn't do nothing but holler at me to do it. Like Josephine."

"Josephine?" said Keith. "What's she got to do with anything?"

"Long before you come she was up here," said Franklin. "She was a kid and I fetched and carried for her when George worked the mines and Leah preached."

"Well, I ain't no baby," said Keith. "I'm six years old and can take care of myself."

"No, you can't. Neither could any of you. Whoever come here I took care of. I took care of them that lived here, too, all the time."

"You got to go, Franklin. That's what Mommy said."

"Ruby don't know nothing."

"She does, too," Keith protested. "It's what Vida and Jake told her."

"Well, see if I care!" shouted Franklin. "I ain't no loony."

"I don't see why me and Mommy can't stay up here!" Keith said, his voice nearly a wail.

"Me, neither," said Franklin miserably. "Me and you and Ruby."

They sprawled quietly at the far end of the barn, too enervated by the heat to quarrel anymore. Yellow bars of light stretched through the dimness. Keith watched the dust floating in the sunlight and waved his hand back and forth, swirling the spores and dust motes. Franklin stared glumly up at the rafters, at the nests of paper wasps and mud daubers.

He was disoriented. He could think through the rest of the day and tomorrow. He knew what would happen because he had gone through it with Daddy James, but after that? When the old man died, he still had work to do. He had Deborah to look after, cut stove wood for, haul coal for, plow for with the borrowed mule, to hoe and heft for. He toted for her from Barker's Store. But after tomorrow? He'd been threatened with the State Hospital for as long as he could remember, and the mysterious notions he had of the place filled him with so much terror that he forced them from his mind. He didn't want the blinding lights, the pounding in his head. Why was it Keith was going away? But Ruby needn't. He could do for her. He hated the old woman; he hated Deborah. He should be glad she was dead, but his mind was confused. He was angry, not glad, and his heart was burdened, not lightened. He missed, already, the source of his life's misery. He missed seeing her lash out at him with her hand, hearing her shout and call him names, because her eyes would sometimes scare over, because she looked as if she were the one struck, and he would then be secretly glad, almost as if she had touched his face, not hit it, and called him a sweet child, not a bastard moron. Ruby came to his mind again, and all

215

the strain and weight dropped away, as when near sleep his own body was a comfort to him, curled on itself and warm, as when the cold of the kitchen eased into warmth when he built a fire and the frost-ferns melted from the windows. He heard a mockingbird's song so pitched and trilling that he shivered in delight. The mockingbird was in the dogwood tree at the back of the barn. He listened and dozed, and after a while he said to Keith, "I'm hungry."

In the heat of late afternoon, Ruby avoided the living room, leaving it to Vida and the lingering guests, to Reverend Bledsoe, who lit the candles in the tall candelabra at the head and foot of the casket, who murmured condolences and patted Vida's shoulder with an oily palm. The house slowly cleared. Ruby sat on the porch, watching the heat lightning beyond the mountains. Keith ran up to her and grabbed her arm.

"Franklin says he ain't going to the asylum," he whispered.

"I know it, honey, but he'll have to go, most likely."

"That's what I told him, but he got real mad. He said us three ought to live here together."

"I've been thinking I wish we could, too, but I don't see how. Anyway, if you been quarreling, you ought to make up with him."

"We did already. He said he was hungry."

"You can take him a plate of food," said Ruby, getting up.

"If I do, can I sleep with him in the barn?"

"Yes, but you better take blankets. Might rain, get chilly."

Keith hurried back to the barn with two plates of food. "Here I am, Franklin!" he called out. "I got ham and chicken, greens and potato salad and white cake. Mommy says I can stay all night, too. I'll get some blankets."

"I need me some water," said Franklin huskily.

"I'll get it."

"Take that feed pail over there."

Keith rinsed the pail, scouring it clean with his fingers because he loved Franklin and wanted to care for him. He carried it back, brimming and sloshing over. "Thank you, Keith," said Franklin, gulping to wash down the cake. "You really going to sleep out here?"

"That's right, just you and me."

"We'll go above when it's cool."

Keith leaned against Franklin, the sound of his gurgling belly in his ear. "Will Great-granny rot like the cat?" he asked.

"She'll be in her coffin."

"I know that. I don't mean will she get dirty. I mean, you know, like that cat in the weeds."

"No," said Franklin. "They do something at the funeral parlor."

"Do what?"

"I don't know. It makes them last forever."

"Oh. Well, that's good. Franklin, is your pecker big?"

"Big as what?"

"I don't know. Mine's little."

"That's because you're little."

"I guess, but can I feel yours?"

"Reckon so, but just for a minute," said Franklin.

Keith unbuttoned his overalls and reached inside. He was surprised at how small it was, like a dead mouse with its soft, slippery skin and soft body. Keith squeezed it a few times in his palm until it grew, he estimated, to the size of a banana. His curiosity satisfied, he pulled his hand away, and Franklin buttoned his overalls.

"Will mine be like that?" Keith asked.

"Don't see why not," Franklin answered.

A couple of days back when Deborah was carried to the undertaker's, Ruby had changed the sheets and made up Deborah's bed, but no one was expected to sleep in it. She took Franklin's bed and Vida catnapped in the big room in the back throughout the night, getting up several times to make sure that someone was sitting up with the body. Jake had gone home, of course, but Wade had returned and stayed until near daybreak, dozing on the couch when a fitful sleep overtook him. Throughout the night, he did take several of the neighbors home. Vida appreciated his solicitude and thought it was a damned shame that he wasn't Ruby's man. Once, when she got up, she asked him if he wanted a cup of coffee. He nodded and they went to the kitchen.

"You think this Waugh family is crazy?" she asked. "Or at least me and the Leah part of it."

"No," Wade answered carefully. "Just full of spirit, maybe."

"That's the truth," said Vida. "We've given everybody up and down the creek a fight to chew on for awhile. But, you know, I don't really give a damn. And Wade, I apologize for that remark I made about you being...well...a little overweight. I wish you hadn't of heard that."

"Ah," he said. "Everybody kids me about being fat."

"You're not fat so much as real big, your height and all. And I don't want you to think my fighting with my sister is any reflection on you. She'd drive the Devil crazy."

"I guess she could," said Wade. "She...."

"She what?"

"She's different."

"But you're over there a lot," said Vida.

"Yes I am," he said.

Vida didn't want to push him. She knew that a man would rather cut his tongue out than to talk about problems in bed. "You remember what Leah said about our Uncle Matthew?"

"Yes," said Wade, "but I didn't follow it."

"She was accusing me of sleeping with my uncle, and having a baby by him."

"She what?"

"There's not a word of truth in it," said Vida. "Matthew and Franklin showed up at the same time, and there wasn't any connection in that but pure chance. Leah said what she did out of meanness. I never knew a man before

Jake. But Leah, you see, never had much to do with George for years. Fourteen, to be exact."

"No kidding?" said Wade. "Maybe that explains...certain things."

"Leah isn't good to you like she should be?" Vida suggested.

"Sort of," said Wade. "Don't get me wrong, now. I like Leah. She's a good woman in her own way."

"She has some traits that a person could admire," said Vida. "But you have to keep track of her. Now she's playing at being a loose woman, and there's probably not a grain of truth in it. Ruby, now, is as obvious as the nose on your face."

"William shouldn't have treated her like that," said Wade. "That's not how a man behaves with a woman."

"Some men got the brains of a flea. You're good to stay up here like this, Wade, and Mother's not even your kin."

"Everybody needs help sometimes."

"I'm sure Ruby appreciates it," she said with what she hoped was a broad hint.

The weather cooled during the night, and a long steady rain began to fall, lasting through the dawn and well into the morning, so that the funeral service, off on a ridge beyond the house, was a dismal, muddy affair. Wade's fedora dripped at the brim onto his nose; his black suit clung to his large bulk like a shroud on a steer. Even the ladies' colored umbrellas were depressing. Vida began crying afresh, and Leah sobbed chokingly, which was harsh to Jake's ears, since he had a hangover. Ruby cried silently. Franklin shuddered for a moment as if he might convulse and fall, but the trembling passed, and he merely stood there, glum-looking and dejected. Keith stared wide-eyed, aware of the other gravestones, of the somber wet sumac just beyond the fence, of the sassafras and sapling poplars at the edge of the field, aware of the warm, gray sky, seemingly so low that the rain did not fall but rather that the family walked in rain-clouds to the funeral. He had worried about the pall bearers slipping in the mud, and now he worried about their having to lower the coffin into the grave, which looked to him awfully full of water.

Reverent Bledsoe, with a pall bearer alongside holding a black umbrella, stepped to the head of the casket. Keith was too distracted for awhile to listen, but then began to hear: *I show you a mystery: we shall not all sleep, but we shall all be changed in a moment, in the twinkling of an eye, at the last trump: for the trumpet shall sound, and the dead shall be raised incorruptible, and we shall be changed. For this corruptible must put on incorruption, and this mortal put on immortality. So when this corruptible shall have put on incorruption and this mortal shall have put on immortality, then shall be brought to pass the saying that is written, Death is swallowed up in victory. O Death, where is thy sting? O grave, where is thy victory?*

Keith hardly understood a word of what the minister read from the black book, but nonetheless his neck tin-

221

gled. He felt himself lifted from the ground to the pearly sky, as if he had risen into the clouds, where they glowed with expectant whiteness. When he came to himself, he wondered if he'd had a fit like Franklin. He fingered the tiny bottle of smelling salts in his pocket. Nobody would know he stole it, there were so many of them. He watched the coffin being lowered into the grave, saw it float for a moment, then settle into the muddy water.

After the funeral, confused about what to do for the rest of the day, Ruby sank into passivity and let herself be taken to Leah's where they sat at the kitchen table, drinking beer. They could decide about Franklin later on. As the afternoon progressed, Keith began pestering his mother about going back up the hollow.

Franklin, alone at the house, sat on the floor of the front porch, squatted and rocking on his heels, his back thudding against the wall. He kept it up for hours, staring at nothing but the gray mist of the day. He moved to the kitchen, where he sat on a chair, his elbows on his knees, gently rocking back and forth, and moaning in a low voice. Late in the afternoon, he heard a car pull off the road and onto the path. In a panic that they might be coming to get him for the State Hospital, he bolted out the back door and into the mountains.

Keith leaped from Wade's car. "Franklin!" he shouted as he ran up the steps and into the house. "Me and Mommy's going to stay up here with you!" The boy meant for the night, for a few days maybe, but Franklin, scrabbling up the mountain side, was too far away to hear.

"God!" Ruby said. "Where is he? We'll have to hunt for him."

Bewildered by the high mountains, for all the years he had lived at the foot of them, Franklin struggled up the ridge till he gasped for breath and his legs cramped. He stumbled onto the narrow flat, and sighing thankfully, dropped to his knees on the moss. A shard of rock pierced his leg just below the kneecap, and he screeched in pain. He howled like a dog, and if people could have heard him, cold shivers would have raised the hair on their necks, goosebumps on their arms, since ghosts were with Franklin, Deborah and Daddy James in the gray fog of evening. He rose and struggled to the top of the ridge. A twig lashed across his face. He wept at the smarting pain in his eyes. "Oh god! Oh god! Oh god!" he bawled, spittle at the corners of his mouth, mucus smearing his upper lip. He shuffled on till he reached the mountain peak far above the house. He staggered near the edge of a cliff, its broken ledge disguised by laurel and huckleberry. Directly ahead, a barred owl rose hugely and silently across his path. He screamed, veered sidewise and fell to the nettle-covered rubble below, cracking his skull, breaking his wrist and leg. He moaned through the night, and the day, till dehydration overtook him, and the loss of blood.

Chapter 10

Although she was among her family, Vida felt as if her true guests were the dead: Matthew and Franklin, Daddy James and Deborah. Her interests abided with them. They occupied her thoughts more often than the living, all of whom could go about their business, anyway—Ruby and Leah and Jake—though she was unsure of Keith, since he had a peculiar look in his eyes, but the rest could manage—Beulah, Charles and Della—and of course Danny could, and the grandkids Sally and Luke, even pooty, scraggly Pete. She could divest herself of the living and dwell with the dead, since her memories of them were much more vivid than the adults on the front porch, and the kids out back, realer than the pressures and tensions of the living, who insisted on making their presence known, their self-centered needs and wants, pushing against life, tearing from it what they thought would requite their desires and their maws of selfishness, except maybe Wade, who served and served and got, if he were lucky, a scrap, a bone to gnaw on, for all his effort, because it wasn't the force of his meaty needs or any silly dreams that he approached people with, but his accommodating spirit, the kind of man you loved when all the other was done. Ruby wouldn't have him, or if she did, she wouldn't have him for long, except to fall back on, except as a babysitter while she was out searching for the man who did for her body what was natural to it, which was to make the present so real that neither the past nor the future mattered, that nothing mattered but the flesh and bones she lived in, supported by a dream having little to do with cooking a dinner or caring for a baby. Hers was a precarious dream, a dream that could be swept like a minnow in a flash-flood to the filthy river below, or caught in a slimy pool, gasping to death in a drought.

Wade? Ruby? She was thinking about Franklin. She always saw him as having some work at hand, with a hoe, a skillet, a pail. It was he who served, who made life easy for Daddy James and Deborah, for Josephine when she was up there, and Ruby and Keith. He was the servant, the bastard manservant. Vida wondered why he hadn't actually killed Deborah and Daddy James, and herself and Jake, too, a long time ago. He had just cause. And he had the ax in his hand to use on her. The ax was the image of her punishment, and try as she might, she could not fear or condemn her executioner. Franklin's hands were merely an instrument for carrying out a sentence predetermined before he raised his arms. And she would live with the image of her guilt and punishment until she died. It would rise before her in moments of self-righteousness, or in the moments of helpless need when no one came, no gentle voice or hand against her cheek. She thought suddenly that Franklin's illness was a miracle, not from God, perhaps, but a miracle that must be akin to the spirit. She thought of the many times in her life when she should have been struck dumb to the floor, when a restraining hand should have held her back. If she could have believed in God, she would have thought that Franklin was a child of God. But they were dead, Franklin and Deborah and Daddy James; the blame was at an end, the accusations and defense against them. All that was left was sorrow and desolation, and a cry for mercy from the soul.

And that's what Jake didn't seem to understand, that people suffered and ought to look at the cause of it. She wasn't blaming him because he was a man. Leah didn't look at suffering, either. She danced around it, play-acting one thing after another. After the floozy would come its opposite, not the church this time around, but the county election board or some such thing she could shine or stand out in—and Ruby didn't care much for anything unless it could stop time somewhere around 1938 when she was courting William. She would probably be holding one hand against the clock and the other around her dancing partner till she dropped dead. No. It wasn't because Jake was a man. He was deliberately and blindly self-serving. He wouldn't look at anything that detracted from himself, particularly if he happened to be at fault. Because of his bad conscience, Franklin for him didn't exist as a person but as a retard, and getting him to Weston was a way of proving that the man wasn't human and didn't need to be treated as such. The same with his whoring around on her. Not that he was actually taking this woman or that woman to bed, not that she knew of. What he wanted was to show his independence in front of the men in the Pool Hall, to show that he could flirt and hang out with the fellows, that he wasn't, in other words, pussy-whipped. He would deny doing so, of course, if she confronted him with it, just as he would deny any responsibility for Franklin. Jake lied to himself on purpose. He muddied his mind so that he couldn't see, except for the picture of himself as a whiskey-drinking, hard-working, coal-mining man with a heart as pure as a roughhouse boy's. To keep that picture, he made himself dumb and cruel on purpose. Leah's voice startled her out of her reverie.

"Lord god, it's worse than a plague of Egypt around here," she said. "I feel like all I done all summer is go to funerals."

"Poor Franklin," said Ruby, "to have to die like that."

"To fall over a son-of-a-bitching cliff in the dark," said Jake. "Jesus Christ! You should of seen him, his leg all twisted back, the blood out of his nose and mouth. God, the flies! And it looked like animals had been gnawing at him. Agh, the horrible green on his—"

"That's about enough, Jake," said Vida. "It's all over and done with. He was found, and now he's laying in peace with Mother and Daddy James."

"I know," he said, "but I hated bringing in the law. All them bloodhounds and I was the one that stumbled onto him."

"It's the last time you'll stumble onto him," said Vida. "He'll never pass by our gate, ever again."

"We did our bounden duty," Leah said sourly, flicking the ash of her cigarette into the yard. She had slowed down on the drinking but had started to smoke. "It sure as hell cost us enough."

"It wasn't so bad," said Jake, "considering the arrangement we made."

"Those acres are in my name," said Vida, and then to take out the sting she added, "Me and Leah's been through all that. Her with the money, and now the house and the thirty-five acres, and me with the forty-two."

"Mother slighted me, of course," said Leah. "Just like she did in life."

"Don't start that," said Vida. "Mother never gave much thought to the either of us. We were the last of the litter, us girls, and after three boys, to boot."

"You going to move up there, Leah?"

"With no electricity! Lord, no."

"Appalachian Power could run you some lines."

228

"I don't know," she said. "We'll wait and see."

"Anyhow, you can understand what I was trying to do getting him into Weston. Deborah was gone one day and look what happened to him."

Jake finally—finally—was able to justify to himself and to anybody who cared to pry into his business why he wanted Franklin in the State Hospital. He wished that he could gloat, but he knew better in front of Vida. Besides, there was something about finding Franklin at the foot of that cliff that took some of the satisfaction off.

"It could have happened to anybody in the dark," said Vida.

"Nobody but an idiot would go up there in the dark," he said.

Vida realized at that moment that she would leave Jake, not today or tomorrow, but soon enough she would leave him.

Life was filled with shocks.

Deborah had said she'd urged her to marry Jake. Well, she had spoken highly of him, but Vida had assumed that the decision was pretty much hers to make, and she had made it. She hadn't felt that she was sacrificing her life to Franklin. She had assumed that Franklin would come with her, if not to live, then at least to visit every day and stay over whenever he wanted to. But Jake denied him; he wouldn't even let the boy in the yard. That was the shock of Vida's life, and she nearly miscarried with Beulah because of it, and Beulah was born premature, anyway. What could she have done? She was a young wife; she wanted to make her marriage work because it was what a person did, and she couldn't bear the thought of returning to that houseful of hate up the hollow, not after the lovemaking and the early happiness with her beau. But then, there was the gate. It was easy to salve her conscience by placing the blame on Jake, and she had done so for years. But it was her own weakness that was at fault, her own giving the lead to a man. She had learned better over the years than to believe that a man's word was the law, that coming from his mouth it was somehow right. But learning that truth was too late for Franklin.

And Deborah saying she didn't want Vida to sacrifice herself to a child that wasn't even her own, when what she was really doing was punishing Daddy James through Franklin, and however much Daddy James might have suffered, Franklin was the one the real pain was inflicted on. Vida was going to leave Jake. Maybe she would go somewhere way off, like Cleveland.

"I shouldn't of gone to Mommy's," said Ruby. "I should of stayed with him."

"Why?" said Leah. "He wasn't your keep."

"We didn't leave you alone when Daddy died," said Ruby, "or alone at Granny Deborah's, either. Why would we think that Franklin was different from us, that he wasn't human?"

"It's done," said Vida. "You should have given more thought, but it's done. Don't blame yourself. You was just living up there."

"It was my home!" Ruby cried. "It was my home."

"I know, I know," said Vida, reaching to touch Ruby's hair, to stroke her shoulder. "All of us miss Mother something terrible."

How could Ruby shout *no*, no it wasn't Deborah, not her but Franklin she was talking about, Franklin for whom she would have given up the Ecco Pool Hall. He was the one like a child, and also like a parent who waited on her and cared for her, which her mother never did and her father couldn't. He was gentle as a woman but bodily a man. He made her safe and sweet and excited. He brought tenderness into love, and when he was wild in lovemaking, he was giving himself, not thrusting himself upon her as a thing different from herself, but a forgetfulness in which all distinctions vanished. Later, she would touch his face, his eyelashes, his lips, and remember when he lay on the kitchen floor, when his contortions passed and he was no longer disgusting and ape-like, but handsome and beautiful in sleep, when his shape and form were free of torment, free of Deborah and Daddy James and all bastardy, and he was a man. Ruby shuddered and sighed deeply.

"In all this mess," said Leah, "Ruby's got the short end of it."

"I'm doing fine," she said. "I just wish I'd done better by Franklin."

"It's your own self you got to think about, now," said Leah. "Not only did you get no allotment checks, but now you got to hand Keith over to them Brouseks."

"It's the best thing, Mommy. You know that."

"When's Margie coming to get him?" asked Vida.

"Tomorrow."

"That soon!?"

"She wants to get him settled in before school," said Ruby.

"Well," Leah grumbled, "good riddance to bad rubbish is all I can say about that father of his. Maybe somebody will drown his ass in the Pacific Ocean."

"Ever time I think of him slapping Ruby around," said Vida, her voice rising, "my blood boils all over again. I should have blowed the son-of-a-bitch's head off!"

"Shit, yes," said Leah. "Ruby would of been a soldier's widow and got a pension."

"Good thing I wasn't here," said Jake. "He probably would be dead. By the way, Ruby, you know Ralph quit at the mines. He ain't showed up for two weeks. I heard he went to Boone County. You want me to ask around?"

"No," she replied. "He's not worth nothing."

"It's a piss-poor time to be finding out," said Leah.

"It don't matter," she said. "The baby's by William. By the time it's born, everybody will know it's William's."

"Smart girl, Ruby," said Leah. "Maybe you can make him pay up, yet."

"It's not that," she said. "It's the Brouseks I'm worried about. They're taking Keith, and ain't no need them thinking the worst."

"The hell with them bohunks," said Leah. "You can come live with me and Josephine. Wade's promised to help."

"You found yourself a regular gold mine in that Wade," said Vida.

"I found myself a tub of lard," said Leah bitterly, "but he does help out."

"You thinking of marrying him?" asked Jake.

"Lord god no!" she answered. "And another thing's for sure. I ain't going back to preaching."

"We have the Lord to thank for that," said Vida.

"Now don't you start, Vida," said Ruby. "You all made your peace after the fight at Granny's wake."

"How long you figure it'll last, Ruby, a week?" said Jake, smiling.

"It'll last as long as you keep your trap shut about it," said Vida. "And what's wrong with Wade, anyhow? I sort of got used to him."

"He's all right," said Leah. "He's got a good job at the mine office, and he ain't the kind to fall asleep on the railroad tracks."

"I think Wade's real nice," said Ruby.

"I never rendered his lard," said Leah.

Jake went gape-mouthed, then laughed till he choked.

Ruby snickered. "Mommy!"

"Maybe I'll sic him on you, Ruby," she said. "Maybe you could trim the fat, get down to the meat."

Jake laughed again, and so did Vida. Keith, at the back of the house, paused to listen. He decided that the racket was laughter and not a fight. He continued. "Dearly beloved, we are gathered here at the river—"

"It's a creek," said Sally. "It's not a river, it's a creek."

"Shut up, Sally!" Luke shouted at his sister. "Now you go on, Keith, like before."

He extemporized as he went along. "We are gathered here to wash in the blood of the Lamb, to wash our sins away. Luke, whenever I stop like that, you're supposed to say *amen*, and Sally and Pete are, too. Jesus is our salvation. Now, you all say *amen*. Jesus climbed on the cross. He rolled away the tomb. Jesus is bringing in the sheaves, Hallelujah! Who amongst you children will be the first? Who will rise from the water white as snow?"

"I will," said Luke, stepping forward.

"Bless you, brother," Keith intoned, taking Luke by the arm and leading him into the water. "Now, you put one hand on your nose. You take ahold of your wrist with your other hand. Watch me. Yeah, that's right. And what I do is hold your arm and the back of your neck. You ready?"

"Yep."

"Luke Hapney, I baptize you in the name of the Father, the Son, and the Holy Ghost, Amen!" Keith pushed the boy backward, dunked him and yanked him up. "Hallelujah, Brother, Hallelujah!" he shouted.

The children leaped around on the bank like monkeys, shouting and squalling. Sally, who was prissing about, could hardly wait her turn. And Pete, the youngest, was beside himself.

Hearing the commotion from the porch, Vida rushed to the back yard. "Good god!" she shouted. "I thought somebody was killed. Can't you all play Cowboys-and-Indians like normal kids? If your Great-granny Deborah could see what was happening she'd switch you till your legs was raw, you blaspheming like that."

"She'd have to catch me, first," said Luke, strutting.

"She can't catch nobody," said Sally. "She's dead."

"Don't get smart-ass, Sally, or none of you. And come on out of that water. The air's getting cool. Josephine will be here soon. She's going to look after you while we're in Ecco."

"You going to the Pool Hall?" asked Luke.

"Where do you think we're going," said Vida, "to the Methodist Church? Of course we're going to the Pool Hall. You kids would drive anybody to drink. We'll just be gone for awhile."

"Sure," Luke jeered.

"Don't get sassy, now, or I'll take a switch to you, my-self. Lord, Sally. Get that green slime off your ankles."

Vida herded them over the outcrop and into dry shorts and tee shirts. Josephine arrived directly, the

235

pouty sixteen-year-old, with acne still blemishing her sullen face, her slouching body still in the grip of baby fat. She carried a movie magazine, its pages wrinkled and dog-eared. Her favorite star was Rita Hayworth.

"There's stew for you all, Josephine," said Vida. "It's on the back of the stove. Just rinse the bowls when you're done. We'll do the dishes in the morning. The kids don't need a bath. They been in the creek all day. Just keep them from tearing down the house and strangling one another. We'll be back after while."

Josephine waved with barely disguised hostility as the grownups drove away. Her feeling was that she should be going with them. She definitely was not some knock-kneed babysitter whose Saturday night they could ruin. Piss. All she had to look forward to was Danny coming in, and who in the hell knew, god-dammit, just what hour of the night that might be. The grownups could even get home before he did. What with her luck, he was probably out jacking off with his buddies.

As Keith stood by the fence and waved to the retreating adults, he knew that Vida's *after while* meant some time later, but nobody knew when. He walked around the house and over to the outcrop. Grownups didn't mean anything but what to watch out for. They slapped quick, big hands and big faces, big voices that didn't make sense half the time. They set food on the table, poked a washrag in your ear, scrubbed your neck raw, said *go to bed, get up!* Even Ruby did that, his own Mommy. No need to expect her to hug him, not when he wanted it, anyway, just when she was all beery-breath and slobbery, when she didn't look but stared through him, watery-eyed and glazed like she was hit over the head, when she smothered him to her titties and he couldn't breathe. Late at night, always late at night. In the daytime she hollered at him or acted like she was deaf and blind, like she didn't see him or hear him. Like he wasn't there. Just don't ask for nothing. Just watch out for them. He broke a beech twig and gnawed at the sweet, green film of bark. Poopie! he spat. What was wrong with playing revival? He missed Franklin. The feeling was awful. He wanted to hit somebody and he wanted to cry.

Luke yelled at him; he had chicken feathers sticking out of a rag band around his head. Josephine screamed at them from the back porch. She slopped stew into bowls, sent the plate of corn bread clattering onto the table, and filled their milk glasses past the rim. The children ate in a bickering sort of misery, and afterwards squabbled at a game of tag, roughhousing until Pete, reduced to blubbering frustration, curled up on the couch and slept. Sally, who was raised to a pitch resembling hysteria because the boys kept breaking the rules, also retreated to the living room to comb the tangles out of her doll's hair, managing as she did so to make the doll even more bald-headed than it was before. She cooed and fussed over it until Josephine, thumbing through her movie magazine, was on the point of gagging. Left to themselves, Keith and Luke swore eternal brotherhood by pricking their fingers and mingling their blood. They came indoors just past dark, and Josephine decided it was time to scare the shit out of them.

"You all know, don't you, that Franklin's ghost walks the ground up there at Granny Deborah's?"

"No he don't," said Sally. "Besides, it's our *Great*-granny Deborah."

"Yes he does," said Josephine. "Everybody's seen it. It's so bad that he's stirred up Deborah herself."

"Oh, shit, Josephine," said Luke, "that's just a dumb-ass story to scare kids with."

"No it ain't. I swear it. Besides, you don't know everything. Did you know, after Franklin fell over that rockcliff in the dark, that he laid there half alive for four days? Did you know that the wolves ate at him? And vultures, too? Why do you think the coffin lid was down? Nobody could look at a man that had his face eat away. And, now, the wolves show up at the graveyard, howling all night, especially in the full moon, because they want to finish eating him."

Keith shivered violently, and even Luke paled. Sally ran to sit by her brother, clutching at her doll. Josephine smirked with satisfaction. "And now his ghost, screaming and moaning through the night, has stirred up Deborah. The two of them sit in the living room of that old house, the moon shining through the windows, and when the moonlight hits them you can see them talking to one another. They shine like glowworms and lightning bugs. You can see what they look like, Franklin with his face gnawed away, his jaw bone and his teeth and his eye sockets showing, and Deborah all moldy, with worms in her hair, and coming out of her mouth and eyes. They sit there wailing and moaning, two green ghosts, while the wolves prowl around outside in the moonlight."

"They won't come down the road, will they?" asked Sally, terrified.

"They've not been known to, but who can tell about ghosts? Franklin might be coming for some flesh to put on his face. Deborah might be coming for the family that made Franklin run away."

"We didn't make him run away!" wailed Sally.

"Our families was going to put him in a loony bin. The—"

"Franklin wasn't no loony!" Keith shouted. "He was a retarded epileptic. Mommy said so."

"Shit," said Josephine. "He had bats in his belfry. Now he's got bats flying through his body. He might take it out on us. We're the children. I can just see him, now, floating down the road, empty eyed, glowing green."

"I'm sleeping with Luke!" shouted Sally.

"That's a good idea," said Josephine. "Keith can sleep with Pete."

"I want to sleep with Luke and Sally!" Keith exclaimed.

"You can't. Remember what I said about the ghosts? If you stir up a racket, Franklin might hear you."

"All right! All right! I'll sleep with Pete."

She got them to bed in a flash and settled down to wait for Danny, thinking about the downy hair just sprouting around his dick, and how she would wrestle with him and jack him off while he had his thumb in her pussy, since it was not her notion of a good time getting pregnant like Ruby was again. Stupid sister of hers. She didn't even have a man who'd keep her. Danny came in around ten, and she pounced on him at the door, scaring him nearly witless, tumbling him to the floor, squealing and giggling over him. He grunted with unexpected pleasure as she reached between his legs.

The din roused Keith, who had settled his fears about Deborah and Franklin and was nearly asleep. His first panicky thought was that the ghosts had come, but his mind cleared as he listened to the tittering and snickering. He sighed and turned back to Pete, gathering the three year old in his arms for comfort. He slept for about an hour before the nightmare came into his mind. He saw Franklin standing before him very clearly, his face mutilated as Josephine had described it, but his expression was not ghastly so much as inexpressibly sorrowful. His jaw worked. What was left of his mouth opened and closed, but the words were faint, garbled. Keith strained to his utmost, concentrating, listening, but couldn't understand a word. There was only the grief in Franklin's mouth, the bleakness and suffering in his eyes. Deborah was plucking at his sleeve, trying to talk to him, but he wouldn't look at her. He looked only at Keith. The boy moaned and gasped, pulling away from Pete and lying on his back. He raised his arms and waved them before his face. He woke up.

And he saw the shadowy room, the doorway a gray yellow, the dresser and bureau dark, the flimsy curtains a veil through which a creature could leap and tear at his chest, ripping him open with its claws and fangs. It would come to him from the darkness of the window. No one could help him. He turned instinctively to Pete.

Later in the night there were voices, but he was asleep again. "Ruby! Watch where you're going. Jesus. You didn't drink that many beers." Vida was talking. "Go on and get to bed. Bumping into things like that you'll have a miscarriage or something. I got to clean the kitchen. Damned stew on the floor, and spilt milk."

Rather than bed, Ruby had staggered to the front porch where she sat on the edge with her feet on the top step. She was thinking of all the men she had attracted, yet how it all come to nothing, how she obeyed her body, how she drifted and floated with it as the only truth in her life, the only sweetness and freedom she knew, yet it betrayed her. It had dragged her to the tedium of children and a coal camp house. William hadn't provided anything. His steely blue eyes pierced through her and beyond, into a future as alien to her as a January sky. And no one would expect anything of Ralph; his attention was on the thing between his legs; he wasn't much more than that, and mindless to everything else, especially to the juke box and the music which Ruby loved, the dalliance which made a romance of the body, which lifted sex to a state of longing for the ideal of it.

She couldn't have taken Franklin to the Pool Hall. He would have had none of it, and neither would the family, no lounging around drinking beer with him and talking. And the few times she had flirted with him, as she had once done with the men at the hotel, she ended up feeling ridiculous and ashamed of herself. And how could she have taken care of him? She would have had two children, really, the child on the way and Franklin himself. And so far up the hollow. Being in bed with him had been wonderful, but she wasn't sure she liked the innocence of it so much, and the lack of difference between him and her took the edge off, took the challenge away. And she didn't care all that much for being in control, and for feeling sad as often as she did with him afterwards, as if lovemaking were a compensation for pain instead of a joy in itself. She needed the real difference of a man, and to be carried away.

But God, not with Wade. She had listened to Vida and Leah hinting, in spite of the fact that Vida had called him Wimpy Wade at the fight during the funeral. Jake had laughed about it later. And Vida was right. He was fat and already going bald, and he sweated. He was nice, but he was a bucket of lard with body hair. Ruby shuddered, thinking that she would have to please him. What else could she do?

A few minutes later, Vida came to the porch. "Damn messy kids," she said. "Ruby, you oughtn't linger out here all night."

"Here, sit down," said Ruby. "I was thinking of William. God. If only he hadn't been so mean. He beat me worse than a dog. And Ralph ain't nothing, not worth a moment's thought, and William screaming about him as if I paid the man any more attention than I would a rock. William killed ever sweet thought in my head. He left me bruises for the rest of my days."

"Well, I don't know about the rest of your days," said Vida, "but I do know one thing. I'll be leaving Jake, and pretty soon, too."

"You will?"

"Yep. Reckon I might go to Cleveland. You can come with me."

"Maybe," said Ruby, "but I doubt it. Lord. What would I have done with Franklin if he had lived? Mommy wouldn't have signed those asylum papers. She'd have kept him up at the house just to spite Jake, but she wouldn't have taken care of him. I know her. And you couldn't have signed, either. You wouldn't have agreed."

"I don't know, Ruby. I'm leaving. I might have."

"Franklin was so good me. Lord god, what have I done? Why did I leave him up there all alone? He'll never forgive it, never from his grave. I shouldn't have gone with you all to Mommy's. I should have stayed with him. I miss Franklin!"

"Ruby, what are you saying? Don't tell me that you and Franklin—"

"And what did Mommy say about you and Matthew, that Franklin was yours and his, and that—"

"Leah's meaner than a snake. She's also full of shit. Me and Matthew never touched. Mother made him sleep in the barn, though she petted and made over him enough. I think she was half in love with him, herself. And I had the baby. I had Franklin to pet on. I was fifteen, Ruby! I was just a girl. And Matthew made over Franklin. He was so brimming with fun, so different from Daddy James that I couldn't take my eyes off him. I loved him, all right. I loved Matthew, but it was all a dream. I've thought about it for twenty-eight years, Mother and Daddy James, me and Matthew and Franklin."

Vida sighed deeply and lit a cigarette. She was thinking that they weren't actually real—Matthew and Franklin—that the past was like a fog on the ridges while she was at the clothesline with a tub of bank clothes to hang; the past was like the creek out back, the ferns and moss and pure creek water while she was standing at the kitchen sink, up to her elbows in grease. She needed to get away from the hollow. Danny was nearly grown, and he was her last.

"I didn't think Franklin was yours," said Ruby, "but whose was he? Did he really come from Grandpa James? Julie Beth Dickins could have lied. Franklin's father could have been anybody. What if Matthew was the father?"

"No," said Vida. "Matthew never went over the mountain like Daddy James did. Not that I know of."

"Then somebody else, another man besides Grandpa."

"You want to think that the Dickins girl was a whore and nobody knows the father of the child? What do you care, Ruby, unless you'd been sleeping with Franklin and wanting to think he wasn't your kin. Who's the father of that child you're carrying?"

"Oh, Vida! I don't know. It's Ralph's or William's or Franklin's."

"Jesus god! What a mess."

"What have I made of life, Vida? What have I made of it?"

"Ruby! If Franklin wasn't Daddy James's, then Mother suffered twenty-eight years for nothing. She was burdened with a hate and a guilt she should never have had to remorse over. She could have loved Franklin as...I don't know...as an orphan or something. Instead she made a slave of him out of hate. He did everything up there, Ruby, everything. You were there. You saw it. And when he was a boy I abandoned him. I let Jake rock him from the gate, from my own yard, my own house. And then I drove him into the mountains. It was me! I let Jake threaten him with the asylum. I killed him. I as much as pushed him over that cliff."

"All of us were in it, Vida. Granny and you and me. I left him up there alone. I abandoned him! And look at me, now, letting Keith go to the Brouseks. He'll know I deserted him, too! Soon enough he'll know, and he'll never forgive me. Oh, god! Sometimes I think I want to die."

Keith awakened to hear the two women sobbing on the porch. The grief came faintly to him, unlike the wailing when his Grandfather George was killed on the railroad track, when he had clung to Deborah and wept, and different from his Great-granny Deborah's funeral when he went somewhere in the clouds as the preacher spoke.

"It's not true, Ruby," she said, "that nobody knows who Franklin's father was. It was Daddy James. I saw Daddy James in Franklin's face when he raised that ax against me."

"Of course he'd look like Grandpa James. He was raised by him."

"It ain't no good, Ruby, you trying to tell me that Franklin wasn't Daddy James's. Why would he bring Franklin home if he wasn't his?"

"It's something Keith said."

"Keith?! What's Keith got to do with it? He's a child."

"What Barker said to him at the store."

"Barker's a sanctimonious old goat. He can't sell you a pound of bologna without wrapping it in a Bible verse. What'd he say?"

"The way Keith told me, it was something like Jesus didn't have no earthly father but Franklin had so many he could as well have come from the sky."

"Barker needs to keep his trap shut," said Vida, though she was startled and a little irritated, since the thought that Franklin was a child of God was what had come to her mind earlier that evening.

"You'll have to live with whatever the facts are by yourself, since I ain't making no judgment," said Vida. "Mother and Daddy James both ignored him as if he weren't there, as if he were a ghost, so it's no wonder we might think he came from out of the blue. You know what I'm talking about? You ever notice when he was about to do something mean he had a fit? It's like God touched him on the shoulder and stopped him. I could use a hand like that on my shoulder. All of us could. There'd be less causing of pain in the world, less guilt and sorrow and regret. Maybe God called him back, back to the place where he belonged, since it's sure enough he didn't have a home down here. That's what Mother would say, that he finally made it through the gate. Not my gate, that's for sure."

There was a long silence.

"I feel like I'm dying," Ruby whispered.

"You ain't going to die," said Vida as she pulled away from the niece she was embracing, "not even if you feel like it and think you are. You're going to do what Mother did, what I'm doing right now and have been doing for twenty-odd years. You're going to suffer guilt and remorse, just like Mother and just like me, but you'll have that baby. Franklin will slip to the background of your mind, and so will Keith. You'll have that baby and you'll find a man."

Ruby sighed despondently, and as they sat at the edge of the porch, their feet on the top step, Vida was thinking that the clouds would pass. The rain would fall, and the sun shine, the creek would flood its banks and settle back, the weeds would flourish and die, as would the vines on the fence, the trees, the ridges and the mountains. It was only when the fog lingered, when it blew through the pines, when the rain streaked down the window panes, when the snow lay on the greenbriers like wedding lace, when it lay on the black limbs of the oak like a heavy mind, it was then the heart would ache, when the memories crowded and the tears welled, when cries for the guilt and sorrow rose, for what was done and couldn't be undone, and for what was suffered.

"Come on, now," she said as she rose and went into the house.

Keith waited and waited, but nothing happened, no heavy sagging of the bed as she got in, no tired arm pulling him close, no beer breath and sloppy kisses on his cheek, no snuggling close to her chest, no heartbeat, no snoring. He got mad, and then curious as to where she was. He was very frightened, but he slid away from Pete and snuck into the side-room where Josephine was sleeping. His mother wasn't there, or with Sally and Luke, either. He knew she wouldn't be in Jake and Vida's room. Maybe the kitchen. But she wasn't at the table. Bitterness and hatred rose in his chest. The forbidden word *Fuck!* formed on his lips. He went to the living room, though he knew she wouldn't be there, and was startled to see his Granny Leah on the couch. He heard a hiccupping sob from outside. "Aie!" he squealed. His hair stood on end. It was Franklin!

"Keith, honey, you up?" Ruby asked from the porch.

He went to the screen door. "Mommy? Is that you? You about scared me to death. What are you doing out there?"

"Nothing. Having a cigarette. You got to pee or something?"

"No," he answered. He opened the screen door partway and looked. The porch was dark except for the far side where light from the kitchen window shone on it and the grass in the yard. The light made the grass a sick green.

"Why don't you come here, darling?"

She was sitting on the steps. He could see the glow on the tip of her cigarette. He walked out on the porch. It was dew-cold and he shivered. He sat beside her and she put her arm around his neck. But it felt dead, not a comfort but a burden, and his shoulders were cramped.

"Why didn't you come to bed?" Keith asked. "I was having a dream. A real bad one."

"You were? I'm sorry, honey."

"I dreamed about Franklin," he said. "I was real scared, but I was sorry, too. He couldn't talk, you know, in my dream. And Great-granny was there, too, clear as could be."

"Such awful things have happened to us," she said. "But maybe you've dreamed it all out of you, now, and can sleep. I'll have to bed down with you and Pete tonight. Your Granny Leah is on the couch."

"I saw her. Did she throw a fit down at Ecco again?"

"No," said Ruby, smiling. "Not this time. I was just sitting here thinking."

"What about?" he asked. "Franklin and Great-granny?"

"Not just them. I was thinking how I ain't made a life for myself and you. I've messed everything up."

Keith was silent. Her arm was sagging on his shoulder and he could hardly breathe. He shifted uncomfortably. She took her arm away and hugged herself.

"Jesus," she said. "Ain't a good man anywhere, none that I can find. They all went to war and didn't come back."

"Fighting them Krauts, you mean?" he asked coldly. "And them Japs?"

He wished he was fighting them. He stiffened his back. He sat rigidly with his eyes wide open while his mother sobbed. She slumped in misery until her head was at his shoulder, her dark hair against his neck. He sat upright and stared ahead, but he couldn't shut away the sound of her sobbing, or the spasms of her body against his. Abruptly, Franklin's face appeared before him, and Deborah's as she pleaded, as she tugged at Franklin's sleeve and wept. He was confused. It was as if his dream came back to him and he were wide awake, so frightened that he thought he was going to die. A creature was tearing at his chest, some black animal he couldn't see, sharp white claws and fangs he couldn't see, fiery eyes he couldn't see. Then, and he wasn't sure how, because the animal's neck and shoulders blocked his view, he saw Franklin's gnawed and pecked-at body, his mutilated face. Franklin was turning toward Deborah. He took the woman who wasn't his mother into his arms. The black animal vanished. Keith shuddered and sighed; tears dampened his cheeks. He turned and stroked his mother's hair, and patted her shoulder.

"It's all right, Mommy," he whispered. "It's all right."

She hugged him and pulled him onto her lap, oblivious of his victory over the creature, the animal that would have torn the heart from his chest.

****

When the morning light came, he leaped out of bed, pestering his mother into a groggy wakefulness, though it was much too early. Pete, too, was up. He was in the other room, jumping up and down on Luke and Sally's bed. Vida screamed in an undertone from the kitchen, telling him to behave himself and come eat his biscuits and gravy. She'd beat every kid on the place black and blue if they got Jake up with a hangover. Ruby, who never understood

251

how Vida could drink all evening and still get up at the crack of dawn, slipped into her dress and staggered into the kitchen. Keith was nervous, fearful that he wouldn't be ready for his Aunt Margie, and so put on the outfit his mother bought him, a white shirt and tie, a brown cotton-twill suit and new oxfords. She had even bought him a hat. He felt like a store dummy, and starched stiff. She told him that he could wear the suit to church on Sundays. He strode into the kitchen feeling awkward and self-important, holding out the tie for his mother to fix around his neck.

"My lord, look at that!" exclaimed Vida. "It's little Lord Fauntleroy!"

"He does look good, don't he?" said Ruby. "His Granny Brousek will be proud of him."

"Sure she will. He's the spitting image of them, any-way, what with that shock of white hair and them blue eyes. Mary Brousek will think she's got another boy."

"And I can come visit you all any time I want, can't I?" asked Keith.

"Sure you can, baby, just any old time you want," Vida answered, glancing at Ruby, knowing that they'd be lucky if they saw him at Christmas.

"You better eat a bite, honey," said Ruby gently.

"I ain't hungry."

"Sit down, Keith!" said Vida. "I'll get them other hea-thens in here in a minute. Lord, I'll be glad when school starts."

"Me, too," said Keith excitedly.

"It's only three weeks till some peace and quiet around here," she said, setting a plate of bacon, biscuits and gravy before Keith. "Grandkids, god! I feel like I'm raising a whole new set of children. I only wish Pete was old enough for kindergarten."

"Their going to school just means we're getting old," said Ruby, who wished that her Aunt Vida didn't talk so loud.

"Shit, Ruby, you can't be twenty-five, yet, and I'm practically twice that."

Ruby and Vida drank their coffee, and Keith, after nibbling for awhile, decided that he was pretty hungry, after all, and finished off his meal by sopping the gravy with chunks of biscuit, washing them down with cool, buttery milk. Vida's Jersey at last had gotten over her taste for wild onions. Luke and Sally came to the table, and there was the usual hubbub of breakfast. Pete whined for his milk in a bottle, which irritated Vida, since the child was already three years old. Ruby went to change her dress and comb her hair. She finished Keith's suitcases and set them on the porch. Leah stumbled sleepily into the kitchen, and directly Jake made his way to the coffee pot. Josephine, of course, would sleep till noon, and so would Danny on his cot on the back porch.

After breakfast, when Leah and Ruby had helped do up the dishes, they gathered on the front porch, lounging away the Sunday morning, chattering, drinking coffee and smoking cigarettes. It was a late August morning, early enough for a lingering, dewy coolness under the maples, though the day would turn dry, dusty and hot. Keith sat on the front steps, too worried about dirtying his new suit to join the kids at the tire swing. Ruby sat beside him and put her arm around his shoulder.

"You'll like your Aunt Margie, Keith. She's a real nice woman, and your Grandma Mary is the sweetest thing you'll ever meet."

"I wish I didn't have to go. I wish we could have stayed with Franklin."

"I know it, honey. I wish we could have, too, but he's gone, now. And just think, you'll get to see your Daddy when he comes home on leave."

"Will you get to see him, too?"

"I doubt it, baby. You know he's divorcing me. He thinks they could raise you better than I could, and he's probably right."

"I don't see how come."

"Well, I didn't have much to say about it, but I guess the truth is they can offer you more. I ain't got nothing, you know, no job or no home."

"How come my Daddy didn't take us to California?"

"Keith, darling, that's too long and complicated, but you remember us fighting out there in the road, the day of the bad storm? You wouldn't want us doing that all the time, would you?"

"I reckon not."

"But I loved your Daddy, and I love you, too."

"I love you, too, Mommy," he said, choking on his tears.

"God," she said. "I ain't got nothing and I'll never have nothing."

That realization washed over her like the mud and trash in a storm. She was wrong in thinking that Franklin couldn't be a man. If only she hadn't left him after Deborah's funeral, if only she hadn't wanted to drink beer and talk, always talk, always the babbling family, always that closeness which he couldn't be a part of. If only she had stayed at the house. If only Deborah hadn't died. There was more real pleasure of an evening, sitting with her and Keith and Franklin in the living room, than there had been at the Pool Hall. Deborah would read from the Bible, Keith beside her, watching her finger as it moved across the page, asking her a hundred questions, and Franklin listening, looking at Ruby and smiling, a calmness about him that made her heart ache with sweetness and desire. She loved Franklin. She was drowning in the loss she'd caused, hopelessly blaming herself, grieving for what there was no hope for. He was dead forever.

A car drove up, a dilapidated Ford, and a pleasant, blond young woman got out and came to the gate. Keith looked up and saw his Aunt Margie, his father's sister, and an ill-humored, surly-looking man behind the wheel. Keith stood up quickly and walked to the porch, standing beside his suitcases. Ruby got to her feet, straightened her dress and wiped her eyes.

"Is that you, Margie!" shouted Vida. "Mercy god, I ain't seen you in years! You're pretty as a picture."

"Why, thank you, Vida, and it seems life's treating you good, too. Hello, Ruby. And how are you, Mrs. Dingess, and you, Jake?"

"We're all fine," said Leah, attempting to be as pleasant as was possible with a foreigner.

"You all come in and have a cup of coffee. Is that John in the car? Tell him to come on in."

"We can't, Vida. I got the baby asleep in the back seat."

"You got a baby?"

"A boy, Lanny, three months."

"Lordamercy, I must be getting old. I remember you in pigtails."

"You know how time flies. Do you think Keith is ready to go, Ruby?"

"He's ready. He's got his things all packed."

"He sure looks good in that suit. His Grandma's itching to see him."

"Keith," Ruby called to him, "come and meet your Aunt Margie. You seen her as a baby, but you don't remember."

Keith lugged his two suitcases into the yard and stood awkwardly before his aunt. She took his hand, and holding it between her own, looked directly into his eyes. He glanced and saw nothing mean or disobliging in her face. She just looked curious, friendly and worried.

"It appears he's ready to go," she said.

"I guess he is," said Ruby, leaning to hug him good-bye, tears forming in her eyes again.

Keith hugged his mother, but his mind was racing ahead to the unknown people who were his father's, and to the schoolroom, both of which excited him with possibility and dread. It was only at the gate, when he looked back at his family in the shadowed light on the porch—at Ruby and Leah, Vida and Jake, at Luke and Sally and Pete gawking from the doorway—all of them stilled as in a black-and-white photograph from a moldy cardboard album, crumbling with age and gnawed by silverfish, that he sensed what was happening to him, that he was departing from them forever. They had become his past, in a place as far away as Franklin and Deborah.